A BOY AT THE LEAFS' CAMP

A BOY AT THE LEAFS' CAMP

Scott Young

McClelland and Stewart

McClelland and Stewart Limited
The Canadian Publishers
25 Hollinger Road
Toronto, Ontario
M4B 3G2

Canadian Cataloguing in Publication Data

Young, Scott, 1918-
  A boy at the Leafs' camp

ISBN 0-7710-9090-0

I. Title.

PS8547.095B69 1985   jC813'.54   C85-098444-0
PZ7.Y68Bo 1985

Printed and bound in Canada

A Boy at the Leafs' Camp

CHAPTER 1 ◼

When Bill Spunska got off the bus with his dad's old brown suitcase, he stood there for a minute looking this way and that, wondering where he was to go next. He had been around bus depots only a few times before but this was like all of them. There was the smell of diesel fumes and a dusty hurried atmosphere, full of people – sitting, standing, walking, reading, talking. The loudspeaker called another incoming bus and people moved to board it. The official letter from Toronto Maple Leafs said to report to Peterborough this Sunday night, ready for camp to begin Monday. He was 1,500 miles from home. Suddenly he felt every mile of it.

There was no mistaking what he was or where he was going, with the size of him and his skates slung over one shoulder while he carried his light raincoat and his father's suitcase in the other hand. A middle-aged woman behind a cigarette counter had been watching him. "You for the Leafs' camp?" she called.

Bill took a couple of steps toward her. "I'm

supposed to go to the Empress Hotel," he said. "Could you tell me where that is?"

She pointed back over Bill's shoulder. "Down that street, left one block, right one block, and you're there." She looked at him curiously.

"Never played junior around here, did you?" she asked.

He shook his head. She said, "Didn't think so. I know 'em all who came in here. Never missed a game, I didn't. Who are you going to play for this year?"

Bill swallowed. "Leafs. I hope."

She laughed. Bill had to smile with her. Peterborough had a junior team of its own, one of the best. So she would know the huge jump it would be for anyone of his age, unless he was a famous junior, right into the National Hockey League. And at that, Bill knew a little more than she did. She was assuming that he'd been a junior somewhere. Actually, he'd never played higher than high school. When she finished laughing, she sputtered, "The Lord hates a pessimist!" Then she turned to sell something to a man at the counter. Bill started out of the depot in the direction she had pointed.

The city streets were busy. The September evening was warm. some of the strollers looked as if they might have been at church. The streets were crowded with full cars – weekenders coming here, or heading for Toronto or other cities. As he walked along, glancing without much curiosity into store windows – jewelry, office supplies, a record shop, a pizza place – the woman's incredulous laugh stayed with him. But what was the use of him saying that he thought he would probably wind up back in school or on a Winnipeg junior team? Which he might, he knew. When Leafs handed him the letter (saving a stamp because he'd worked the summer at the Gardens) telling him when to report to training camp, there'd been a note on it from Squib Jackson, the chief scout. Two words: "Good luck!" He'd need it.

Bill felt again the amazement of that night last spring when he'd found that Leafs had decided to draft him. Normally, a player never knew that until it happened. But this wasn't normal. He was still in high school. No other club was likely to draft him except as a dark-horse throw in, late in the draft. But Jackson had persuaded his boss, the owner of the Leafs, that Spunska was too good to miss and should be drafted in the fifth or sixth round. Jackson also knew that Spunska had to improve his skating, was worried about debts incurred during his mother's long illness, and was planning to work full-time that summer to help out. So Jackson had put it all together: arranging a skating program and a summer job in Maple Leaf Gardens that would help the Spunska family exchequer. He'd worked in the gang cleaning the Gardens after rock shows, wrestling matches, political meetings. He'd painted seats and floors. Lived in a boarding house near the Gardens with never a spare moment to feel homesick. That treatment had been a gamble on him that he'd never forget.

In some ways he would have liked to go to university. But he wanted the career in hockey more. He and his parents had come to Canada from Europe. His mother and father both were Polish. All had had the same urge, the fight to get established in their new country. Bill had found acceptance faster than either of his parents. When he picked up the puck and started his big move, the people in a rink didn't care whether he came from Winnipeg or the moon. They just stood up and yelled. He had never owned a pair of skates until the year he started to school at Northwest. Now here he was at the training camp of the Toronto Maple Leafs.

He turned the corner to the left swiftly. This was busier, the main street. Walked one block. Then he turned right and crossed the street. Ahead was a neon sign saying Empress Hotel.

There was a bit of a lump in his throat when he pushed through the swinging doors and took a look at the lobby. Four or five men were sitting around in big chairs, smoking and reading. They all looked up without much curiosity until they saw his skates. Then a couple of them spoke in low voices to one another. Probably they were trying to figure out who he was. Bill grinned. Some day they'd know. He hoped.

Across the lobby, at the little enclosure with the sign above it which said "Rooms and Information," a red-haired girl was watching him. Pretty. He walked toward her. "For the Leafs?" she asked.

"Yes," he said. She looked awfully young. Seventeen, maybe? Eighteen?

"What's your name?" she asked.

Bill told her. She ran one rather stubby finger down a long list of typewritten names. "Room 309," she said. From a rack behind her she took a key and handed it to him, smiling at him brightly. "There's a sign there by the elevator that you should read, I guess," she said. When Bill turned away, he saw her scrutinizing his name again, with her brows drawn together as if she was trying to recollect if she had ever heard it before. Bill couldn't help grinning, again.

Taped to the wall beside the elevator just above the call button was a single white sheet of paper which looked like this:

TORONTO MAPLE LEAFS

Medical tests will be given to all players in the hotel ballroom beginning at 9 a.m., Monday. There will be four doctors in attendance. All persons reporting to camp – repeat – ALL – will go through this examination.

Monday routine: Breakfast, 7:30 a.m. Medicals, 9 a.m. Lunch, 11:45 a.m. Report to rink by 1 p.m. to pick up equipment and skate. If you have a car park on hotel lot and leave it there. Players will walk to and from rink.

There was no signature, but as Bill pushed the button marked "up," he grinned again – the excitement a little higher. He had read quite a bit in the last year about Pokesy Wares, the Toronto coach. He'd seen him on television often. There was a word that Bill had read in some write-up that fitted exactly: truculent. There was always this bit of a chip on his shoulder. When he had taken over the Leafs they had been in last place. They'd never been out of the playoffs since. There was that all-business feeling about that notice by the elevator.

As the elevator arrived, the girl called out his name – "Mr. Spunska!" – from the desk a few yards behind him. He turned. "I forgot to tell you, you'll be rooming with Tim Merrill," she said. "He won't get in until tomorrow. And if you see Benny Moore up there, will you tell him to call his sister?"

He scarcely heard the last words. Tim Merrill! Did he imagine it, or did she keep her eyes on him and then smile at his reaction! Tim Merrill! He'd been one of the best of the Leafs ever since he turned pro. What a break! What had that girl said about Benny Moore? To call his sister? Benny Moore – that was a familiar name . . .

When Bill emerged at the third floor, it was into a kind of noise he had never heard before. Yet somehow he recognized it. When he had made the decision that he was going to be a professional athlete, he'd thought ahead that night, sleepless in bed, to the year after year of training sessions and then six or seven months of hockey a year, all as part of a team. A team meant this. Boys. Men. He could hear them now. Young voices singing with radios. Singing against radios. The sound of showers running. A thud and a shout, "Wait till I get you on the ice!" An answering voice, "I'll go around you so fast it'll take you a week to get your underwear untied!" Burst of laughter.

Along the hotel corridor a young man backed partly through a doorway, looked at Bill, and said in a loud and polite voice, "Why, hello, Mr. Wares!"

There was instant silence. Four or five heads cautiously appeared in open doorways. Then one of them called back into the room behind him, "Nah! It isn't the coach, it's another new guy."

Bill smiled. Lugging his father's old brown leather suitcase in one hand and his skates in the other along the hall, he looked for door numbers.

A young man with crew-cut fair hair was watching. "What room?" he asked.

Bill said, "Three-oh-nine."

"Down there," the boy said, jerking his head toward the other end of the corridor.

Several of the doorways were open. Bill glanced at each one, just a glance. In most of them two or three boys, all looking a little older than he was, were sitting around in sport shirts and slacks. Room 309 was five doors from the elevator. Since Tim Merrill wasn't supposed to get there until sometime tomorrow he was a little surprised to find his door open, too. And he could see some feet on a bed. He paused at the door to make sure it was the right number and then put his skates down. He tapped on the door once, picked them up, and entered.

On one of the twin beds was a large and muscular young man. Bill was six feet. This boy seemed even bigger. And he wasn't Tim Merrill. Merrill had fair hair. This one was dark, with square and regular features. He had a pillow bunched under his head and was lighting a large cigar. Without moving, he took the cigar out of his mouth and said, "Hi, kid, who are you?"

"Bill Spunska."

"Where you from?"

"Winnipeg."

The other boy looked at him thoughtfully, puffed on the cigar, and took it out of his mouth again. "You weren't with the Monarchs, were you? Not when we played them in the play-offs, anyway."

Bill put his bag and skates over by the unoccupied bed, shaking his head. On the street outside the cars had their lights on now in the rather dusty dusk. Bumper to bumper, going home after the weekend. "I played high school," he said.

The other sat up in bed. Some ashes dropped off his cigar. He brushed them off onto the floor. "High school!" he said, then "Oh, yeah! You're the kid Leafs drafted straight from high school. I remember now!"

The incredulous tone of voice irritated Bill a little. There'd been a man in the bus depot, a hockey fan. He couldn't miss Bill because of the skates. The man had asked him a series of questions and it had ended with that same ejaculation, "High school! Oh, yeah, I remember now – that surprise in the draft!"

Then, on the bus, same thing. First the driver. Then another man. This second man had said, rather scornfully, "I never heard of a kid going pro straight from high school!" As if Bill was lying, or something. In fact, there had been the same doubting note in all those voices as there was now in the voice of the young man on the bed.

"That's right," Bill said shortly. "High school." He had given all the information he was going to for a while. "What's your name?" he asked.

The boy on the bed considered this question for several seconds. He sat up on the edge of the bed and stared at the end of his cigar. "You don't know who I am?" he asked finally.

"No," Bill said.

"I'm Benny Moore," the boy said.

There was something curiously watchful about the way he spoke. Not particularly aggressive, but alert, watching for a reaction. And immediately, of course, Bill remembered. He would have earlier, downstairs, except that the idea of rooming with Tim Merrill had knocked everything else out of his mind.

"I know you now," Bill said noncommittally. The cigar made a little more sense now. "The girl on the desk said to ask you to call your sister."

Moore said, "Oh, her."

Bill said, "Are you in this room?"

Moore said, "Does it look as though I'm in this room?" There was an edge of sarcasm in his voice.

Bill said stolidly, "You know what I mean. I was told I'd be rooming with Tim Merrill."

As Bill spoke, he thought there was a flash of something in Moore's eyes; suddenly, across the hard, brash expression, something like envy or admiration, or both. Admiration for Tim Merrill?

"I forgot to pick up my key when I came up the last time," Moore said. "This door was open because the maid was in the room, so I just came in here to stretch out. Thought I might see Merrill, as a matter of fact."

It struck Bill as a little strange that anybody who wanted to see Tim Merrill would come and park himself on a bed and smoke a cigar and wait for him. But then Moore isn't shy, he thought. Bill would have stood around for weeks waiting for Merrill to speak to him.

"Now I hear that those big wheels on the Leafs don't have to get in here until tomorrow if they don't want to," Moore said. "It's just us poor little juniors and," he said with a rather hard look at Bill, "high school kids that have to be here on Sunday night. The Leafs will be up in their big convertibles tomorrow morning in time for the medical."

Moore got up to stretch. He was an inch taller than Bill and broader in the shoulders. He smiled, but the smile was twisted a little.

"I wouldn't mind coming up here in a big convertible myself some day," Moore said, sitting on the bed again. He looked at Bill. Again the brash note was in his voice.

"I guess it must have given you quite a start there for a minute if you thought they'd put you in with Benny Moore," Moore said. There was sort of a challenge in his voice.

"I'm here to play hockey," Bill said. "Not to worry about who I room with."

"I'm here to play hockey, not to worry about who I room with!" Moore mimicked in a high voice. He grinned again and lay back on the bed. He puffed on the cigar and the smoke rose above his head. "Well, when we're working out, keep your head up: I hit pretty hard."

Bill raised his suitcase to the unoccupied bed and began undoing the straps.

"I hit pretty hard myself," Bill said.

From the corner of his eye he saw that Moore had sat up again, with a smile playing around the corners of his mouth. "You what?" Moore said.

Bill looked over at Moore. He knew this was

baiting, and more or less harmless. But he'd had this feeling sometimes before, that a position had to be taken. When he got that feeling, he simply took the position. "I hit pretty hard myself," he repeated.

He thought about Moore. The reason everybody knew Moore's name was not particularly for his hockey ability, although he had a lot of that. In the junior playoffs last spring Moore had been suspended for shooting a puck at a referee when given a penalty. The puck had hit the referee in the face. It had taken ten stitches to close the cut. That suspension hadn't yet been lifted. Bill had been reading one of the Toronto papers Saturday. There had been a story about who was coming to camp with the Maple Leafs. One paragraph in the story had read:

Among the prospects is Benny Moore. His suspension for injuring an official in the junior playoffs last year – when Moore played for Peterborough – is to be reviewed at the end of September. Leafs obviously believe enough in his ability that they are willing to give him three weeks of training time in hopes that his suspension will be lifted at the end of it. His conduct at training camp probably will influence the eventual disposition of his case by hockey authorities. To put it bluntly, if he toes the line, he'll probably be okay. Otherwise – OUT!

"I will be looking forward to the first time you hit me," Moore said from the bed.

Bill knew he was two years younger than Moore. Bill also had heard that there was something in Moore's background that at least might explain his attitude. He'd been brought up partly by grandparents and partly in foster homes. Bill's own idea of him, reinforced by this first-hand meeting, was that he had a reputation he felt he had to live up to. But Bill was too tired right now to play games. He'd worked at the Gardens late last night after the wrestling show, then hadn't slept very well, from excitement.

"Why don't you grow up, Moore?" he asked, in a hard straight voice.

He hadn't noticed that the doorway had filled with three large young men just as he made that remark. Their shout of laughter startled him.

One yelled back along the hall so that both Bill and Moore could hear him, "Hey, you guys! The new kid, you know what he just told Moore? 'Why don't you grow up, Moore?' he said to him!"

And a distant voice called lazily, "Let us know the date of the funeral."

CHAPTER 2 —

When the telephone rang the next morning, Bill didn't know where he was. He sat up with a start. Then he saw the empty bed and the light blue sky outside the window and he knew. His heart gave a great jump. First day in camp!

"Did I wake you?" the voice said. "It's Squib Jackson."

"Hello, Mr. Jackson!" Bill said. In his mind he could see the round, kind little man with the bristly mustache, Leafs' head scout.

Bill didn't have a watch but that notice by the elevator had said breakfast at seven-thirty. He could hear phones ringing along the hall. The desk must be getting all the hockey players up at the same time.

The scout said, "I thought maybe you'd like to have breakfast with me and two or three of the others. Get you acquainted a little."

Bill said that sounded great.

"See you downstairs, then."

Bill got cautiously out of bed and pulled a cord that hung along the side of the venetian blinds at the window. The blind ran up a little. He didn't want that. Then he found the right cord to close the slats a bit. When he'd fallen asleep the night before he'd had one instant's consciousness of a flashing neon sign on a restaurant across the street, an instant when he thought it would keep him awake and he should get up to close the blind. He must have gone to sleep four seconds later. People were beginning to move on the street below. He could see the long slant of the morning shadows, hear a distant auto horn.

The shower felt good. He'd never had a shower in his own room before. They had an old high bathtub at home. The showers in the dressing rooms at the rinks he'd played in were always communal affairs. As many yelling, slippery, soap throwers as could squeeze in, did so. It was more of a competition to keep from getting soap in the eyes, or frozen, or scalded, than it was a shower. He couldn't help a grin when he stood under this one, all by himself, hearing the sounds of others stirring all along the hall. First day! He wondered if he'd get on the ice today. And suddenly the full impact of it hit him. He, Spunska, eighteen and a half years old, about to go out on the ice with men like Tim Merrill, Rupe McMaster, Otto Tihane, Anson Oakley – all those names he'd heard on the broadcasts, had seen on television at Pete Gordon's place.

That made him think suddenly of Sarah, Pete's sister. He'd sure missed her this summer. Funny how just seeing that nice red-headed girl at the hotel desk here had made him think of Sarah. She'd been away working as a waitress at Banff all summer, to make money to help with university. He thought of how he'd felt going to see her the night he left, back in June. When he'd finally had to say good-bye, she'd hugged him right in front of her family, prompting Pete to remark, "If that blood rushed up to your neck and face any faster, William, it'd be two feet over your head before you could catch it!" He wondered what kind of a sister Benny Moore would have. And shook his head.

Bill let the water rush over his cropped dark hair and down over his shoulders. Then he stepped out, picked up a towel, and dried himself. After a minute's thought, he turned back and washed the tub. He didn't know for sure if the maid did that or not. But he wouldn't want Tim Merrill to come in here and find the place in a mess.

Cleaned his teeth.

Looked straight into his own eyes in the mirror, and said, "You're the luckiest guy alive!"

Rubbed his hand over his chin and knew he didn't really have to shave, he'd shaved yesterday, and then shaved anyway.

When he was dressed in black loafers, grey

slacks, white shirt, tie, and blue blazer, he looked at himself. Okay. There were some things he wouldn't have to be told. Ever since he'd known he was coming to this camp he'd been listening every time anyone talked about the National Hockey League. One thing he'd heard was that when you were a pro, you dressed and acted like a pro. He was sure going to try.

First man he met in the hall was Moore. Moore was in a golf shirt, a new windbreaker, black slim trousers, pointed shoes. "I give you," said Moore to the world at large, "Bill Spookski, one of Winnipeg's ten best-dressed high school hockey players!"

He took a cigar from his shirt and took the wrapper off.

"Spunska," said Bill.

"Spookski," said Moore.

A tall young man wearing spectacles and with freckles and a sandy complexion had heard the voices and came to the doorway of the next room. Bill recognized him. It was Morey Mansfield, the left wing who'd been rookie of the year in the NHL two years ago. He looked from Moore to Spunska and back to Moore again, and then disappeared. He'd said nothing. Moore said nothing more, either, lounged there lighting his cigar as Bill walked along the hall toward the elevator.

At the bottom, it gave Bill a warm feeling to see Mr. Jackson in the lobby. Someone he knew! The little scout jerked his head at another boy with him. "Jiggs Maniscola," he said. "Bill Spunska." They shook hands. "Just waiting for Merv McGarry," the scout said, and looked at his watch. "We'll go in." He called to a very tall man sitting in a big leather chair, "Hey, Pat! If you see that fathead McGarry come down, tell him we've gone to eat, will you?" The man called Pat said he would. "Pat, he's one of my scouts," Squib explained. "Joint's full of them."

They climbed a few steps to a mezzanine and then went through a swinging door into a big room set with long tables covered with white tablecloths. At one end wall was a large blue maple leaf. Underneath were the words, STANLEY CUP CHAMPIONS. Under the maple leaf two women in white uniforms stood behind a long table loaded with jugs of orange juice and tomato juice and several big covered dishes. The scout led the way. Bill could see he was trying to make them feel at home, leading the way so they would know the next time. It helped. Bill picked up a plate. "Juice? Take your choice," the scout said. He took some and put it on a table nearby, staking a claim to that place. Bill and Jiggs Maniscola did the same. Then the ladies piled their plates with ham, bacon, sausages, scrambled eggs, toast, bran muffins.

On the tables were pots of jam, honey, marmalade, a jug of milk, corn flakes. When Bill sat down he thought he'd never seen a breakfast like it.

"Gosh, in the old days," the scout said, as they ate, "and I mean, maybe twenty years ago, it was sure different. They'd bring in maybe three or four rookies to camp in a good year. They'd room together three or four to a room, while the regulars would be two to a room. Treated 'em differently in just about everything. Not like that now – who are you with, Bill?"

Bill chewed, swallowed convulsively, and said, "Mr. Merrill." The scout looked at him, startled. "Mister who? Oh, Tim Merrill!" He swallowed hard once himself with a little grin playing around his mouth.

Both Bill and Maniscola knew he was amused by the "Mister." Maniscola said, "I'm with, ah, Ron Stephens."

"Call him Mister if you want," the scout said suddenly, and they all laughed. "If it'll make *you* feel better. It'll certainly make *those* guys feel better." After a pause, he went on. "The whole setup now is fixed so that people get to know one another, fast. Mix 'em up in the rooms, rookies and veterans. Same in the dressing rooms. Same on the ice for the first few days. Then if one of you kids gets called up in the middle of the season some time, you come in at least knowing a few people. Helps keep down the butterflies the first time you skate out there in the big rink."

The thought of it was enough to make Bill's food stick in his throat. Just those few words had made him see it, as plainly as if it had happened. And suddenly he felt a little . . . well, almost silly. He remembered his big words to the lady in the bus depot last night, that he hoped he'd play with the Leafs, this season. What a hope – thinking that out of fifty or so players, most of them with pro experience and the rest some of the best juniors in the country, he, Bill Spunska, straight from high school, would have any chance to stick with the Leafs. He shook his head and then felt better. Well, they'd drafted him, hadn't they? Couldn't take that from him!

He watched the players coming in to breakfast. Quite a few knew one another from junior or other camps. Merv McGarry, the veteran Leaf utility forward, came in then and hurried over, apologizing. "Hey, Spunska!" he said, when they were introduced. "Hey, Jiggs!" he said, taking Maniscola's orange juice and draining the glass. "Hey, Squib! What's good up there? I'm starved." As he approached the table he was saying to the lady nearest, "Steak for me, dear. Medium well." She gave him eggs.

The scout grinned, watching him. "Talks all the time," he said. "Very funny. Good for morale. Not a bad hockey player, either. Some nights."

Bill, drinking a final glass of milk, wondered what the scout would say about him if he were describing him to someone else. "Spunska . . . yeah, not a bad kid. . . . Of course, you can't expect a kid right out of high school to . . ."

He was finished. "How about going for a walk, Spunska?" Maniscola asked.

The scout laughed. "Now, there's the kind of a guy! Knows darn well you're going to be walking to and from that rink twice a day, about a mile each way, four miles a day not counting golf or whatever, so what does he do, goes for a walk!"

Bill was on his feet, ready. The clock showed only eight o'clock. They didn't have to be back for the medical until nine. Through the window he could see the lovely bright fall morning, leaves turning on trees a block away. He thought of the guys back at Northwest. Grouchy DeGruchy. Pete Gordon. Stretch Buchanan. Pincher Martin. Horatio Big Canoe. Benny Wong. The whole team went through his mind in one long flash. How could one guy be so lucky? How come he was here, instead of one of them?

On the way out, they met Benny Moore coming in. Bill saw him first, for just an instant. In that instant, if there was an identifiable expression on Moore's face it was uncertainty. He looked almost scared. Then it changed. A cloud of cigar smoke came out. Moore swaggered past, without a look.

Maniscola said, "Benny Moore."

"I know," Bill said.

"You'd wonder how two such different people could come from the same family," Maniscola said, as they passed the hotel desk. The red-haired girl was on duty this morning, too – but on the switchboard. Bill glanced at her and she smiled. He smiled back, just catching the end of what Maniscola had said.

"Uh, what do you mean, such different people?" he said.

"Benny and his sister."

"I wondered about that," Bill said. "What's his sister like anyway?"

"You've seen her." They were at the big glass doors leading to the street. Maniscola jerked his head back toward the desk. "The red-haired one. Name is Pamela."

"His sister!" Bill looked back. She was looking the other way, working at something. All he said then was, "My gosh!"

CHAPTER 3 ■

The medicals were a sort of organized chaos. They were done alphabetically, so Bill found he was in for a long wait. But even that was interesting.

Everywhere he looked, he could see faces he knew from newspaper photos and TV. Peterborough was a little more than an hour's drive from Toronto. Some Leaf regulars had driven up this morning. They must have left early because some were in the ballroom ready to be medically examined by the time the four doctors trooped in and proceedings got under way. At nine-thirty there was a visit from the coach, Pokesy Wares, a small, stocky figure, with not much hair on his head.

He walked into the middle of the room, ignored all the conversations going on around, then suddenly barked, "All right, you guys! I want every one of you to do twenty push-ups, twenty knee-bends, and twenty sit-ups. This'll help pass away the time while you're waiting for some doctor to tell you you've got bubonic plague and send you back to Melville, Saskatchewan."

Half a dozen of the Leaf team, the Stanley Cup winners from last year, set up a loud groan. Pokesy glared at them.

"All right, you Leafs," he said. "You're the hotshots who've got it made and all that stuff. You can do twenty-five push-ups each and show these rookies how the real pros do it."

There were further groans. Bill watched carefully. Every Leaf did the prescribed twenty-five. Looking around the room, Bill noticed that a lot of the rookies went to twenty-five also and some even to thirty.

When Wares was leaving the room, there was a high piping voice from back among the rookies. "I can do fifty push-ups, Mr. Wares," the voice said. "Does that get me a job on the Leafs?"

Near the door, the coach looked to the group of juniors where the voice come from and said, "All right, McGarry. Come out from behind those juniors."

McGarry got slowly to his feet.

"Don't be rude to me, Pokesy," he said. "You know as well as I do that I got you where you are today."

Everybody was listening now.

"I made you famous in every league you ever coached in, and you know it."

The coach laughed and said something that sounded like "Aaaah." And then left.

Maniscola, finishing his push-ups on the floor beside Bill, said, "McGarry is like that about half the time in the dressing room, too. He kids the coach all the time except when it counts. Then he listens like anybody else."

Bill said, "I didn't know you'd played with the Leafs."

Maniscola laughed. "I was only up for five games last November, when McMaster got hurt. Remember? They needed a left-winger for a few games. I hardly got off the bench. I wasn't like Moore. When he was up for three games he was hardly off the bench either, but he wound up with twenty minutes in penalties. At least he got his name into the records."

When Bill's turn came with the doctor, he drew one named Jim Murphy. The examination was quick and to the point – a few questions about whether he had any aches and pains, what serious illnesses he'd had (none) and what non-serious ones he'd had. Then the physical examination – listening with the stethoscope, hitting Bill here and there with a little rubber hammer to see how his reflexes worked.

Dr. Murphy was a tall and youngish-looking man, with a nice slow smile. Everything he did seemed unhurried. As he was checking Bill, he asked how far he'd gone in school. Bill told him.

The doctor asked what his father did. Bill told him what had been big news in their family this summer – his father had been appointed an associate professor of history at the University of Manitoba. He'd been an assistant before that.

"We get them all, I guess," the doctor said. "There are kids here whose fathers are hard-rock miners, salesmen, office workers, just about everything. I think you're the first one I've ever run into whose father is a professor." He looked at Bill curiously. "Did he argue against you wanting to make hockey a career?"

Bill was putting his clothes back on. He remembered the long discussions he and his father and mother had had on this point. "He didn't really oppose it. I don't think it ever occurred to him that I had any kind of a chance to do something like this until it happened. And then, well – he left it to me." What Bill didn't say was that his decision to make hockey his career, if he could, had helped his father decide to stay at the university and take his chance at getting this associate professorship. Until that time, thinking of the money he'd need to put Bill through university, he had been considering very seriously another job that would have paid him a lot more money but would have taken him entirely out of the university life he loved. So in a way hockey had given both of them what they wanted.

At lunch time, the players packed in fairly tightly along the tables in the Leafs' private dining room. There were cold meats and salads, jugs of milk, bowls of fruit on the table, hot rolls and butter. There was nothing in the form of an official statement from the table up near the front where the coach, some sportswriters, and a few of the scouts were sitting, except once when Bobby Deyell, the youthful, athletic-looking trainer, got up and said, "For the benefit of you who haven't been here before, the rink is nearly a half-hour walk away. I'd advise you to be out of the hotel and walking by twelve-fifteen. Three dressing rooms on the south side of the rink have been assigned to us. On the doorway of each is a list of the players assigned to that room. I'll have charge of one, Tommy Nathanson here will have another, and Danny Carsen, the trainer for St. Catharines, will have the other."

Bill had read somewhere that Tommy Nathanson was Leafs' assistant trainer. St. Catharines was Toronto's farm team in the American Hockey League. As Deyell spoke, the two men he mentioned rose briefly. Nathanson was a quiet, older man. Carsen was maybe a little older than Deyell, but still in his twenties.

"When you see your name on a door, go on in," Deyell continued. "Inside you will find your names on pieces of tape stuck up over positions along the benches around the dressing room. At each place will be a pile of equipment, which will be yours for the duration of this training camp. I've tried to make sure it fits by getting your height and weight from Chief Scout Jackson back in the summer time, but if I've made any goofs just go to the trainer in your room, tell him what's the matter, and we'll see what we can do to fix it. There's just one other thing I have to say. The uniforms you will be using are the ones the Leafs wore last year. The chances are pretty good that every rookie coming into this camp will be wearing one of the uniforms that was on the ice last May when the Leafs won the Stanley Cup."

Down a few places and across the table from Bill, McGarry got to his feet and made a noise like a bugle. "Ta-da-da-da-dah da-da-dah," he sang. Then he saluted the big maple leaf behind the head table and sat down again.

Everybody laughed. In the diminishing noise thirty seconds later, Pokesy Wares's voice could be heard from the head table, "That's twenty-five extra push-ups for you, McGarry."

Bill wasn't used to the kind of attention given hockey players at this level. Boys and girls in the younger teens were hanging around the hotel looking for autographs. Bill signed the first autograph of his life. "Quit blushing, kid," McGarry said loud. "You've got to get used to being a big wheel, you know."

The procession to the rink was like a long, disorderly parade along the sunny, tree-lined streets. All walked quite rapidly, but occasionally a little knot of school children on a corner would want autographs. The players would stop and sign. When the coach and a few scouts went by in an automobile, the Leafs called, "Slackers!" after them. A sportswriter with two or three other writers with him drove by in an open convertible. They were similarly jeered. There was a light-hearted atmosphere to the whole thing. Bill wondered whether any of this light-heartedness had rubbed off on Benny Moore.

He and McGarry and Jiggs Maniscola were together. Leaving the hotel two or three other Leafs yelled at McGarry to come with them. McGarry replied, "Some of us old veteran hockey stars have to look after these kids."

Tim Merrill called back with a grin, "I've always thought somebody should be looking after you, McGarry. Preferably somebody in a white coat."

"You thought I was all right when I gave you the pass for the winning goal last May," McGarry called back.

Rupe McMaster entered the fray at that

point. "We're just lucky there was somebody there for you to pass to, McGarry," he said. "If we'd waited for you to score we might still be playing that overtime period." Everyone grinned. McGarry didn't score many goals in a year.

The big rink, about a mile from the hotel, was a new building alongside the exhibition ground. From a parking lot on exhibition property, gates led through a high iron fence to the rink. Those who knew the place walked confidently to the one door that was open. The amateurs followed, and Bill found his name on a door. Inside, Bobby Deyell seemed to have an uncanny memory. "You're right over here, Spunska," he said. "Here, meet Otto Tihane."

Tihane put out his hand and shook Bill's. All the diffidence that Bill had felt last night and sometimes this morning came back, in spades. He felt like a child beside this man. Tihane had played ten years with New York Rangers and had been an all-star several times before he was traded to the Leafs. Bill knew the story pretty well because it had been played up heavily in the papers the first year he had started playing hockey. The Leafs had taken Tihane as part of a deal, sort of a throw-in. Leafs thought he was over the hill and would wind up as a steadying influence on the farm team defence. Tihane had seen things differently. He wasn't ready to leave the big-time. He'd played so well that he had to be kept by Leafs. Two facial scars were noticeable, one that interrupted the line of his right eyebrow, and another high on his cheekbone. He was a tough-looking man, but his voice was quite soft.

"Where you from, kid?"

Bill told him.

"I played there when I was a junior," Tihane said with a grin. "Some time ago." He laughed. "I guess you'd be about two or three years old when I was a junior, eh?"

Bill nodded.

"Well," Tihane said, "I wish I was just starting out."

Bobby Deyell was hustling by with an armful of sticks right then and he heard that last remark. "Would you do it the same way, Ott?" he asked.

Tihane gave a little sniff of amusement. "There'd be a couple of times I was hit from behind that I'd be ready for, if I had it to do over again," he said. "Apart from that I think I'd do it about the same."

For some reason, Bill found this reassuring. He hadn't had to go through the argument about being a professional athlete for some weeks now. A couple of his teachers had argued very strongly that he was wrong to put so much of a stake into anything that depended so much on his physical abilities alone. He knew all that. He'd already decided that in off-season he'd go to summer schools and study. Maybe at the end he could be a teacher. . . . Anyway, he wasn't going to waste the summers. I'll build a career outside of hockey, too, as I go along, he thought. And suddenly he grinned. What do I mean, as I go along?

Just then, in the Leafs' room, Bill's thoughts were interrupted. A boy a few seats down the bench called out to Bobby Deyell to ask if he could borrow a pair of scissors.

"What for?" said Deyell.

Bill could read the boy's name on the tag above his locker: Garth Givens. "To cut the bottom strap out of my hockey stockings!" Givens said, as if to say, what else would I need scissors for?

Deyell looked startled. "What do you want to do that for?" he asked. "Those are good hockey stockings. Nearly new!"

Givens was beginning to lose a little bit of his resolve, but not much. "I always play in my bare feet and with the strap cut out of my hockey stockings," he said. "It cuts into my instep so that I can't get the feel of my skates properly."

The room had fallen silent. Next to Bill, Tihane had his head down, rubbing his fingers along the skate blades, hiding a grin.

Deyell said mildly, "Gordie Howe managed to play for about thirty-five years without cutting the straps out of his hockey stockings. Did you ever think of that?"

Givens said nothing for a few seconds. The grins were rather general around the room now and he could see them.

Deyell said, "Do you mean that out there in Red Deer when it was twenty below you would play with no socks at all in your hockey boots? Not even the strap?"

Givens nodded.

"I'll tell you what you do," Deyell said. "Today is just a skate. You try it with the strap in those hockey stockings today and again maybe tomorrow. And then if you still think that you're being hampered in your attempt to make the Toronto Maple Leafs by the fact that you've got straps in your hockey stockings, I'll lend you a pair of scissors. How's that?"

Well, Givens thought that would be all right, he guessed. Bill took a glance at Tihane sitting beside him and saw the shadow of a smile still playing around the inside of his mouth. He said to Bill in a low voice, "When I first came up, I thought I'd cut the palms out of my hockey gloves, thought I'd get the better feel of the stick that way."

"Did you?" Bill asked.

Tihane grinned. "I never got to find out.

With the old Rangers when I went up, the trainer was a tough old guy that kept telling me for the first five years that I wouldn't be there more than another week and he was blankety-blank sure he wasn't going to let me cut any palms out of any pair of hockey gloves he might have to give some real hockey player some day. I just got used to playing with the palms in."

Deyell went by and caught Tihane's eye and jerked his head sideways backward toward Givens and gave a little smile. Tihane smiled back.

Bill dressed. The long underwear, the athletic supporter, the heavily padded sleeve-like arrangement over his shoulders and then the shoulder pads and elbow pads in his outfit. He had never had equipment anything like as good as this. The pants were just right. There was something good just in pulling the hockey stockings up over the leg pads for the first time and seeing the blue and white of the Maple Leafs' colours on his legs. Tihane was leaving his skates to the very end. Bill did the same, pulled tape over the hockey stockings to hold the pads in place, and then held up the sweater with the number 4 on it. "That's one of mine from last year," Tihane said. "Good luck, kid."

Deyell had been out through the open door to visit the other rooms and have a look at the ice. There had been some clumping of skates outside, but Bill didn't know the ropes well enough to get up and take off. Otto Tihane seemed about ready. Bill thought he'd move when Tihane moved. . . .

Then he saw that Tihane was looking at their skates. Bill's left skate with its battered, soft-looking boot was alongside Tihane's scarred but sturdy one.

"That the only pair you've got, kid?"

"Yes," Bill said.

"What size?"

"Ten," Bill said.

Tihane said, "I'll talk to Deyell and see if there's a spare pair around. Those'll be all right for a day or so until we start scrimmaging, but then you'll need a little more protection than they'll give you."

Bill looked at his skates. They had been new last Christmas, but they had taken a pounding, all right. He knew what they'd cost because the money had come out of his own pay for working after school and Saturdays in the tobacco warehouse. Sixty-nine dollars. He'd thought they'd last for years.

Tihane spoke as if he was reading the rookie's mind. "These ones we use cost over $200," he said. "Might go through two or three pairs in a winter. . . . In a couple of weeks guys from the skate companies will come around taking orders. The club buys them, of course, but not for every man in camp, not at that price. Just for the ones who are going to be with the Leafs or St. Catharines."

Deyell came back and stood in the doorway. "Ice is ready!" he said. "Everybody out!"

Nineteen men and boys stood up, most of them tall on their skates even if they weren't more than normal height naturally. Nineteen stood up. But there were twenty in the room.

"Hey, you!" called Deyell to the one still sitting. "Aren't you going to skate today?"

Some players already had left. Others turned to look at a tall and very skinny boy who was flushing right up into the roots of his hair, a fact that emphasized his haircut. He had a deep tan on his face and about halfway up his forehead, and then his skin was dead white. His scalp also was white at his temples and in sort of a semicircle around his hairline. His haircut seemed to have uncovered a lot of area that hadn't seen the sun all summer. He had a prominent Adam's apple. This bobbed now.

"Gee, Mr. Deyell," he faltered, "I didn't bring any skates."

The players on their way out laughed and kept going, commenting, "Imagine, a guy . . ."

The trainer grinned easily at the youth. "Didn't you think you might need them, to make this team with?" he said gently.

The boy's Adam's apple jerked up and down

again. Deyell was searching that good memory of his, could have looked, but didn't. "You're . . . Butt, eh? Jim Butt from, Melville?"

The boy nodded miserably. "Well, really from Poplar," he said. "That's outside of Melville . . . but I played for Melville." His voice trailed off.

As Bill reached the door and left, with his whole body full of excitement, he could hear Deyell saying, "Sure, sure. Well, now, we'll find you something. . . . What size?"

CHAPTER 4 ▬

Clump, clump, clump. Step after step on the rubber matting leading to the gate to the ice. And then the final one, pushing off with the familiar big cut of the left skate. The players were tall, short, fat, skinny. Some were pelting all out around the ice, laughing, taking the corners in mighty cuts. Others were loafing around, looking at the freshly painted seats and the clean look of this rink. Bill thought it was a beauty. Somebody going by said it seated about forty-five hundred, and that three-quarters of them always were good-looking girls. Some players skated in twos or threes, talking. McGarry, with two other Leafs, was telling a story. At the end, McGarry laughed the loudest, as usual.

On Bill's second circuit, players were still straggling along out of the gate to the ice. He noticed Steve Baldur, who'd been with the Leafs for several years but now was in the minors. The American League was a step slower than the National, but that was where young pros got their seasoning and old pros played out the string. He saw several other faces that he remembered, and it all was part of the building excitement: I'm here. This is my chance.

Pokesy Wares stepped to the ice wearing a blue long-peaked cap with a white maple leaf on the crown. Around his neck was a leather thong to which was attached a whistle. He joined the stream, cutting across it to get to the inside. After half a circle of the rink he stopped at centre ice and stood there watching. Bill circled with the crowd, watching him, wondering what was going through the coach's mind. Last year Leafs had won the Stanley Cup. That was the payoff for the years of shrewd dealing and trading, shrewd work by the scouting under Squib Jackson and the drafting of young players, building Leafs up from last place. Now they were the big team in hockey again. Bill thought: He'll be thinking right now – how do I keep them big? Who is a half-step slower this season, on the way out? Which of these young guys is going to be good enough to step in? Who's going to surprise me? Who's going to disappoint me?

Cut, cut, cut, went the forest of skates, powerful strokes, dainty strokes, the movement of a gazelle here and the movement of a bull moose there. Ahead of Bill was the old defenceman named Buff Koska. He was bald, and his body was a solid thick line from his shoulders to his knees. His nickname, Buff, was short for Buffalo – but nobody called him anything but Buff any more. When he had come to Leafs four years before, the defence had become steadier, and the rise had begun. But last year he had ridden the bench a lot, the fifth defence-man, and the rumours were that now at age thirty-five, he might wind up in the minors.

Bill looked ahead and imagined himself – seventeen years from now, thirty-five. Would he be here? Would he have made the all-stars a few times by then? When people gathered and talk-ed about great games, great playoffs, would anybody be saying, "That was the year Spunska got the winning goal, wasn't it?"

Dreams. He dug in. Passing between some other players, he brushed against the tall kid named Butt, the one who didn't bring his skates.

"I got some," Butt said with a shy grin. Bill involuntarily glanced down at his feet. The skates were battered and cut, and had painted in white on the sides the number of the player who had worn them the year before. Fourteen. That was McGarry, the Irishman.

McGarry saw the number at the same time, going by.

"Live up to them skates, kid," said McGarry

expansively, falling in alongside. "Just tie 'em on every day and turn 'em loose. They've got the old McGarry magic in 'em!"

Bill speeded up. After a few strides, Butt came alongside again. He had a deceptive skating style. In the dressing room, he'd looked lanky and clumsy. Skating, he had power and grace. Without seeming to change his stride at all, he speeded up. Bill went with him, and felt himself straining, seeing in front of him the one big problem he'd lived with for two years: skating. Canadians skated as if they'd been born with skates on. To keep up to Butt, Bill had to scramble and scuffle and push himself. Stroke, stroke, stroke, went Butt's skates, and his head was up, his shoulders even, his motions as un-flurried as if his legs weren't moving at all.

Then Benny Moore went by. He flung his skates up high with every stroke, bending his knee. Bill stayed behind and watched the one flamboyant style and the one economical style – much different in looks, but both effective.

There was a long blast of a whistle from centre ice. Bill looked that way. The coach, taking the whistle from his mouth, was waiting. Some Leafs were gliding up to him and stopping. Two or three went down to one knee. Bill turned in with some of the others. In less than a minute the whole rink was quiet, players gathered around the coach. Almost all of them were bigger than he was but this pudgy figure in cap and windbreaker and ordinary suit pants was dominating them all.

He said, "All right! I've got a few things to say, and some of them I'm going to say once and once only."

Pause for a few seconds while he looked around.

"Three years ago we were in last place. Then last year we won the Stanley Cup. Well, that was last year, eh? This year we've got the same teams to beat, and they'll be tougher for us, because everybody loves to beat the champions. The edge we've got is that we start out knowing that we're the best, and all we've got to do is prove it. Every night.

"A couple of players who were on that team last year aren't here now, and I'm sorry about that," he said. "That's pro sport. But you play your best wherever you go – or you should, because if you don't you won't be a pro long, no matter where you play."

The coach had a rasping tenor voice when he spoke loudly. When he dropped his voice, as he had, it was friendly and conversational again.

"Now, I'll tell you who we've got. We've got most of last year's team. We know what they can do, eh? Most of them are pretty sure to get their jobs back again this year until they prove one way or another that they don't deserve them. Then there are you guys from the minors. We wouldn't have you in the first place if we didn't hope that some season you're going to come to camp and play so well that you just can't be left off the big team. But you ones who don't make the Leafs right now, you know also that you're our next line of defence. When we run into injuries, or a guy goes into a slump, you'll be brought up and you'll get your chance." He paused and looked around. "Finally," he said, "there are the guys who mostly are at our camp for the first time."

This was Bill and the others. He knew it. He looked straight at the coach.

"You're the best we could get in the amateur draft. That's according to the scouts, eh? I don't know about that myself and I hope to find out in the next week or ten days. Right now you have one thing in common. You've all come to us recommended as pro prospects. That's about all you've got in common. You come from different parts of the country, different teams, different coaches, and different styles of play."

Wares looked around among the faces, his eyes going across Bill's face without stopping. Bill thought of the stories he'd read. Wares never had been an NHL player himself. But if that was a drawback in some respects, he more than made up for it. There was a sort of tough, humorous quality to the way Wares spoke. He seemed to be promising them nothing but hard work and likely failure and yet the impulse that rose in Bill was an eagerness to get at it and prove him wrong.

The coach went on, "Now, I'll tell you young guys something else. We don't really expect to get many players for the big team out of you guys. But sometimes we're wrong. Sometimes a guy will come to this camp and play so well that we just can't send him home. Almost every year this sort of thing happens, one or two juniors make us keep them around to see how they look when they are playing against other NHL teams in exhibitions. And once in a while one of them stays all the way. There always is room for a guy who won't be denied."

Wares stopped and turned in a full circle, looking around, thinking. "Meanwhile, you new ones, we aim to teach you as much hockey as we can in a short period. When you get sent home, back to junior, to the minors, wherever, I don't want you to be discouraged. I want you to go and play hockey the way we've taught it to you, improve all you can, and come back here next year and make the big team."

Some newspapermen had grouped along the boards and scribbled now and again, but not all the time. Bill could not understand why they weren't taking it all down. He could feel his spine tingling with eagerness to get going. And it was over. All but the formalities.

"Now I want you to skate for another few minutes," Wares said. "Just to get the kinks out. If any of you need equipment changes, see the trainer in charge of your room. Also, pick out some sticks. Put your name on them and they'll be kept in a rack in your room for when you need them. Tomorrow morning the camp really starts. Tonight there'll be posted by the elevator two lists of names – the first shift hits the ice at eight o'clock, second shift at nine forty-five. Be there, be ready, and good luck!"

The coach turned and a way opened for him and he skated off the ice.

There was a yell of "Yow-ee!" A few more war whoops. Some grins. The skating went on. Bill dug in, wishing it was tomorrow morning.

Later that evening he had his first chat with Pamela Moore. There was no such thing as being lonely in the camp. There were several young players who didn't know anybody, either, and they tended to group together. Butt and Givens had decided to go to a movie and wanted Bill to come along. But he decided to write a letter. The upstairs corridor was quiet. "Dear Mother and Dad," he wrote, and then sat at the desk with the pen in his hand and paper in front of him, staring out of the window. There wasn't really much to tell them, yet. When he wrote to Pete and Sarah later he could tell about Givens wanting to cut the feet out of his socks, and Butt not bringing his skates. Mother and Dad . . . he'd tell those stories to them when he was there to explain in detail. Sometimes it seemed a long way from Poland, where their backgrounds were, to such a thing as a boy wanting to cut the feet out of his socks so he could get the feel of the skates better! Bill laughed and began to write about the trip, the doctor this morning, the big-name players he'd met.

Six pages later, he went downstairs. The red-headed girl was at the desk. When she saw the letter in his hand as he approached, she smiled and pulled open a drawer. "How many?" she asked. "You know, you're the first one to come for stamps. The manager told me to get plenty, that all the rookies would be writing home the first night."

Bill converted a few dollars into stamps. As he was licking one for his letter he said, "You seem to work long hours."

"I get most afternoons off," she said. She had brown eyes, very dark. Nice teeth. Regular features. With a shock, Bill realized that she looked very much like her brother – except for the expression, which made all the difference. She smiled. "I saw you out there slaving away today."

"At the rink?" he said, surprised, and laughed. "We didn't slave very hard today. I wish it had been harder."

"I'm going to go every day I'm off," she said.

She didn't seem busy and she did seem friendly. So Bill asked something he'd wondered about. "Does your family come from here?" he asked. "I mean, I know your brother played here last year, but . . ."

She looked the slightest shade flustered. "I came up here for a few games last November and sort of liked the city," she said. "So-o-o-o-o, there was an ad and here I am!" She paused as if she thought of stopping there. But she didn't. "Oh, maybe I thought a little good advice might do Benny some good, too," she said. "Not that I could get him to listen very often. . . ."

There was a buzz on the switchboard and she had to go. Bill left to post his letter. A couple of scouts in the lobby called out loudly as he passed, "You're too young to be hanging around the best-looking girl in town, there, kid!" Bill flushed. He knew the scouts had intended her to hear, too. He glanced back at the desk. She was laughing. "Thanks for the compliment and go take a jump in the river!" she called to the scouts.

Bill went on out through the revolving doors. She was as natural and pleasant as her brother was moody and unpleasant.

CHAPTER 5 ◼

Bill often thought later that there was a strange fate to the way he and Benny Moore met and all that had happened after that. Suppose he hadn't been in my room that night I arrived, he thought. If there hadn't been that first few minutes, would we ever have riled each other so seriously? Or, no matter what the start had been, would we have tangled anyway?

In the first two days, he didn't think much of Moore. Not as much of Moore, in fact, as he did of Moore's sister. And that wasn't *so* much, either. But it was nice to feel that there was someone he could talk to just casually, passing the time of day. He felt that way about Pam Moore and he seldom passed the hotel desk without stopping when she was on duty.

One morning when he had walked back from the practice, she said, half kiddingly, "How long do you think you're going to stay in camp?"

He said, deadpan, "I guess I'll leave with the rest of the Leafs." He couldn't keep a straight face very long, though. He burst out laughing – and noticed that only when he laughed did she look surprised. "Don't laugh," she said.

Still grinning, he was about to say that from what her brother had said on Sunday night, maybe he'd be lucky to get out of camp all in one piece. But he didn't say it and he did stop laughing. "That's what I worry about," he said.

"Staying?" she asked.

"Staying . . ." he said. "Catching on, somewhere." Even this early Bill was concerned about his survival in this camp. The first couple of days, he was sure he hadn't made much impression. There would be some players sent home at the end of this first week. Would he be one – back in Winnipeg almost before anyone had noticed him gone? He had almost forgotten that Pam was there. She had turned away to tend the switchboard for a couple of seconds. When she came back he was turning away. She saw his expression. When he wasn't smiling, he did look awfully serious. She didn't call after him. Watched him go and thought that sometimes when her brother talked about his future, he looked that way, too. As if he wanted something so much that he was almost desperate. The trouble was, that was Benny most of the time – desperate. She'd tried to tell Benny the things she'd heard so many people say about him – that if he'd just let his ability do the work, hold his temper, be a little easier to get along with, he wouldn't have to worry.

Bill was outside, walking again in the sunshine, before he remembered that he'd walked away without even waving good-bye.

In the early workouts, he and Moore saw one another, but that was all – only because both happened to be young defencemen, and therefore found themselves in the same group sometimes.

On the third day came the first scrimmage. Both Moore and Spunska were on the first shift: eight a.m. on the ice. In the dressing room, Bobby Deyell came in with an armload of white T-shirts and a list and began tossing them out. He tossed one to Bill. Since all the players wore the same blue and white sweaters there'd be no way to tell them apart in scrimmage unless they wore something like this. He was with the Whites for this morning.

When he rose to go to the ice, he picked out one of his sticks. On the stick rack were more hockey sticks than he'd ever thought would have his name on them at one time. The Leaf regulars had stamps bearing their numbers. For instance, Otto Tihane and Bill had picked out their sticks together on the first day. Tihane had just stamped each stick with his number, 4.

The trainer had had some sort of heavy crayon. Bill had printed his name on the handle of each of his sticks. Deyell had told all the rookies how to handle their sticks. "Tape up two or three the way you like them, and keep them in the rack. Then if you break one you don't have to go on a sit-down strike for half an hour getting another ready."

Bill's normal method of taping had been pretty skimpy, he'd realized, watching Otto Tihane. Tihane taped the blade and heel of his stick very heavily. He'd explained, "A defence-man should have a lot more tape on his stick than anybody else. It gets more hard usage. If you're back there in a power-play situation or something like that and your stick breaks, you're in real trouble."

So Bill was taping his sticks now quite a bit more heavily than before. He also put the usual ball of tape on the end of the stick to make it more secure in his hand, less likely to slip out.

There'd been quite a few elements of a school about the first couple of days. The veteran players had helped out the coach in this regard. One day Otto Tihane had taken half a dozen young defencemen into a corner, including Bill and Moore, and simply talked to them. Some-times he had gone out toward the blueline and illustrated a point by doing it. But mostly it was simply talk about the theory of defence – not committing oneself too rapidly, not backing in on the goalkeeper, watching the eyes, knowing who you'd pass to if you got the puck, things like that.

A little later on that morning of the first scrimmage, Bill fell over the boards and sat panting on the bench. He was sweating comfortably but muttering to himself about a play he had just made. It had been a clean three-man break in on the defence. Yesterday they had worked on these three-man breaks without any other players on the ice – just two defencemen and three forwards. So Bill should have known exactly what he was supposed to do. In fact back in high school they had been schooled in the play. Bill could hear Red Turner, his high school coach, speaking: "Don't give the puck carrier a chance to go through the defence. Close up the middle and make him pass. There's always a chance that a pass will go wrong. When you see the pass, go with it for the man who's supposed to receive it. Stay with him. Steer him into the corner and then take the puck away from him. By then there ought to be some wings back-checking and you can get out in front of the net again to cover."

That was the theory. And that was substantially what had been drilled into the young defencemen yesterday. So just a minute ago in the scrimmage it had happened, and what had Bill done? He sat on the bench and leaned his head forward and rested it for a couple of seconds against the wooden rail. What a dope! The Blues' puck carrier had cut into centre. Buff Koska and Bill had been waiting on defence. When Koska had seen how the play was going, with the Whites' forward line trapped down ice and unable to back-check, he'd said out of the corner of his mouth, "Don't move." The centre coming in on them was one of the trickiest of the Leafs, Anson Oakley. He weighed only 160 pounds. The one criticism ever made of him was that he could be knocked off his feet too easily. But you had to hit him first. Bill was determined he wasn't going to move until the pass was made. He wasn't going to be tricked by anybody. Oakley came straight in on him, head up, glancing around to place his wings. Bill watched Oakley's eyes, as he had been taught to do, instead of watching his legs or skates or stick or the puck. But then he caught a movement Oakley seemed to make to his left. He wasn't going to pass! He was going to carry it in himself around that side! Bill wasn't conscious of moving. All he was conscious of was that Oakley seemed to start that way. Bill moved, got his stick out to that side, started in that direction. There was a blur as Oakley cut back in and went between him and Koska. When Bill turned, Oakley was going straight in on goal, the puck at the end of his stick, faking one way, pulling the puck the other and then tucking it behind the sprawling goalkeeper as if there was nothing to this game at all.

Bill looked at Koska. Koska looked at Bill. "You moved," Koska said, without emphasis.

Pokesy Wares, refereeing the scrimmage, skated past Bill. "See what happened?" he asked. That was all.

Bill thought, sitting there on the bench, am I going to have to learn the moves of every forward I play against? Maybe that was it. In high school, he'd certainly known what every man could do when he came in on him. But what had Oakley done? Had he thrown his leg that way and then cut back in? If Bill hadn't moved, would Oakley have gone around him?

A man stopped behind the bench. He was short and stocky, and had his hat on the back of his head. "Red Barrett for the *Star*," the man said. "You found out about Oakley, eh?"

Bill couldn't help grinning. "I sure did."

"Well," Barrett said, "there are guys been in this league ten years and still haven't figured out what he's going to do, if that helps you any."

It did, a little.

His reverie was interrupted by a long blast of the coach's whistle from the ice. "Full change!" Wares yelled. "Maniscola, you take centre with

Givens and McGarry on the wings. Spunska, you go back on with Koska. Moore! Where's Moore?"

Over on the other side of the rink Moore's big frame rose out of the front row of seats.

"On the ice," Wares commanded. "You and Tihane this time."

And that was where it started, the real feud between Spunska and Moore. Maniscola faced off with Rupe McMaster of the Leafs at centre ice. Maniscola outdrew the Leaf and got the puck over to Givens on right wing. McGarry on the left wing lit out for the other end of the ice. "Hey, Barefoot!" he bellowed. Givens simply looked startled. Two or three of the other players laughed. By the time Givens got the pass up to McGarry it was too late – he'd gone in on Moore's side, over the blueline before the puck. Offside.

Bill had to smile. The nickname, Barefoot, was exactly the kind of thing that McGarry would pick up. Givens was smiling, too, now. He still had the feet in his hockey stockings, but he'd be "Barefoot" for a long time in hockey now and he knew it.

As the teams lined up for a face-off at the other blueline, Maniscola got the draw again. Over came the pass to Givens. This time McMaster was on him, poking the puck away. McMaster's wings were sprinting to get with him as he moved in on the defence. Straight at Bill. When Oakley had come in on him before, he'd come in on Bill's side. Now McMaster did the same thing. They put the heat on the rookie, the fellow they figured they could beat.

Bill was determined he wasn't going to be beaten this time. When McMaster came in on him he watched the eyes. McMaster tried to make the same shift and cut-back that Oakley had beaten Bill with before. Bill didn't go for it. When McMaster cut back Bill hit him a good body check and landed him on his pants and there the puck was at the end of Bill's stick.

From then on, it was pure instinct. His wings had been coming back fast to back-check and were going the other way. Nobody was in position for a good pass. Bill broke fast up the ice, carrying the puck himself. He could hear shouts and laughter around the ice and among some of the sportswriters and scouts in the stands. Some of the Leafs were yelling kidding remarks to McMaster for being dumped that way by a rookie. But that only lasted a second or two. Bill gathered speed through centre ice with that shambling, powerful gait that was his style. He could see the wings streaking up to get with him. But none was in position for a pass by the time he hit the blueline. And there in front of him were Otto Tihane and Benny Moore.

He didn't exactly know how he was going to

do this. But up in the stands, at least one man knew. Squib Jackson was sitting there with three or four of his scouts and a couple of the directors of the Leafs. When Bill got the puck, suddenly Jackson sat up. "Hey, watch this!" he called. The others had been carrying on a conversation, watching the ice in a desultory way. They stopped and watched as Bill plunged through the centre-ice zone. "He skates like a ruddy fullback!" one of the scouts complained.

"Watch this," Jackson insisted.

When Bill hit the blueline and there was nobody to pass to, he knew only one way to do it. He just kept on skating. He could see a look of surprise on Otto Tihane's face. Moore and Tihane had played the puck carrier according to the book. They had stayed together trying to force him wide or make him pass. Bill hit Tihane first. He bounced off Tihane and rocketed into Moore. And he could feel the point of his left shoulder hit Moore in the chest and he heard the sudden "Oooof!" as the wind went out of Moore. But hitting Moore gave Bill a chance to regain his balance after the check from Tihane and suddenly there he was, reeling along on his right skate blade, the puck still on his stick, Moore flat on his back and Tihane turning in pursuit. Bill perilously regained his balance. He glanced up and saw the surprised look on the face of Johnny Bosfield, sort of a grin, as the goalie came out to the edge of his crease to cut down the angle. Bill had neither good enough balance now nor the skill to make the play around the goalkeeper that Oakley had made earlier at the other end. He saw a little hole and he let his shot go. At the last instant Bosfield threw up his arm sideways and the puck bounced off his shoulder and over the protective glass into the seats, while Bill, overbalanced completely with the force of his shot, fell and slid scrambling along the ice to crash against the end boards.

When he staggered to his feet, it seemed just as if *that* Bill Spunska, the one that had crashed through the defence and blasted a good shot at the goalkeeper, was gone. In his place was the other Bill Spunska, the diffident high school player from Winnipeg. He'd found that in the practices, the other players yelled a lot and kidded, and now they were yelling. Two or three players, both from his team and the other, were laughing and yelling to one another. Tihane, skating back toward the goalkeeper, grinned at Bill and shook his head. He still looked surprised.

Out on the blueline, Pokesy Wares was standing with a grin on his face. It was more than a grin, really. He was looking at Bill as if he'd never really seen him before. Up in the stands, Squib Jackson was chortling with delight.

"What did I tell you?" he said to the others. "What did I tell you?"

One who'd been in hockey ever since he was a boy, said, "Yeah! But that was all pure luck! Nine times out of ten he'd be knocked down on a play like that and the puck would go to someone coming back and he'd be flat on his ass and his own defence would be short."

Squib Jackson said, "Okay. When that happens, you guys can rib me. I've watched that guy time and again. When he does lose the puck, he doesn't get caught out of the return play very often."

Jackson stopped himself from saying something else. He thought it, though. He'd seen right then the same thing that he had seen in Spunska when he first had noticed the boy out in Winnipeg. This was a quality that he'd seen before in some hockey players. But not many. It was the quality of a man becoming something entirely different once a game began. There was no way of telling, until it happened, the barrelling power that Spunska had when the puck was on his stick and he was going in on defence in earnest.

Bill knew none of this. He was on his feet now. A new puck was being thrown out. The goalkeeper was grinning. "That's a tough shot you got there, kid!" Bosfield rubbed his upper right arm where he had deflected the puck and said, "I think if I hadn't got a piece of it, it would have gone in."

Bill didn't quite know what to say. "Just lucky," he said.

A voice said, a few feet away, "You said it, kid!"

Bill looked. The speaker was Moore, his face about three shades redder than it had been a few seconds before. And suddenly Bill remembered the first time they had met, that Sunday night when Moore had said that Bill should keep his head up because he, Moore, hit pretty hard. And Bill had said that he hit pretty hard himself. Once the instant had gone by, Bill had forgotten it. It came to him now that Moore thought that Bill, the first time he had the puck, had made that play on purpose, to knock Moore down.

Moore said, "Try that again, and I'll take your head off."

Bill started to say that it wasn't intentional. But why say that? This was a game of skating, shooting, and checking, as Pokesy Wares had said. It wasn't a game where you started worrying that you were going to hurt somebody's feelings when you carried the puck through him. Bill hadn't had any intention of embarrassing anybody, and anyway why should Moore be embarrassed? Otto Tihane had been knocked flying on the same play, although he had managed to stay on his feet. All Tihane had done was grin.

As Bill went back across the blueline, the coach skated alongside him. "That was quite a play, kid," Wares said. "But there's no harm in looking around to see how much time you've got. Let your wings get up to you if you can."

"Okay," Bill said.

As Wares skated down into the corner to face-off the puck, tossing it thoughtfully up in the air and catching it, he was thinking: Hey, that kid really took off. He was thinking also of the sudden surge of excitement he'd had when he turned and saw this kid – what was his name, Spunska? – heading up the ice with the puck. He knew that excitement. He watched hundreds of hockey players during a year. That excitement came only once in a long while. Sometimes it came with a beautiful play around the goal, or with a tenacious checking job or a big body check. Sometimes it came from a suddenly recognized surge of power and spirit. When he saw a player who made him feel that way, he never forgot the man's name. Years later, if that man was mentioned, Pokesy would have that feeling. Not many people knew this. It was one of the secrets of the good deals he made. He had in his mind the names of players that roused in him that sudden burgeoning instinct that here was something special. As he dropped the puck and skated rapidly backward to get out of the way, he was thinking, I must be getting a little soft in the head. That kid was just plain lucky to get through the defence with the puck.

Then he noticed Moore was marked with snow from the ice where he'd hit. He was to think later that maybe he shouldn't have said what he did then. But he was an uncomplicated man. He said it. "You can't play defence flat on your behind, Moore," he said. And was startled by the look that came from under Moore's half-closed eyes, a furious glance, as Moore skated up toward the other end where the play had gone.

It was a minute or so later when Moore got the puck. Bill had made a few plays with moderate success in his end at that time, but there had been nothing really very tough to handle. Now here came Moore.

Up in the stands again, Squib Jackson saw what was happening. "Watch this!" he said again. And they didn't argue. They watched.

Bill's rush and Moore's unceremonious knockdown were still fresh in the minds of all present when Moore picked up the puck at centre ice. The difference between his rush and Bill's earlier rush was that Moore's wings were ahead of him. Either was open for a pass. But he kept the puck. His wings slowed at the blueline to wait a split second for him to cross. As he crossed the blueline Bill and Koska were waiting for him. Moore passed to the right wing, Koska's side. Koska started that way. Bill was turning to cover the other wing, who was sweeping in looking for a return pass, when Moore hit him. Bill wasn't even looking for Moore. At the last instant he saw this body hurtling toward him and tried to brace himself but it was too late. Moore hit. Bill knew even before he hit the ice that he never had been hit that hard before. Down he went, sliding along the ice, knocking down the winger he had been going over to cover. Moore had stayed on his feet. Wares hadn't blown his whistle.

"That would be a charge in a real game," Squib Jackson said.

But then all the people in the stands were watching as Koska chased the winger into the corner and Moore moved in toward the goal very fast, ready to take a pass if it came.

Up in the stands, Jackson said for the third time, "Watch this!" As Bill hit the ice and slid he was trying to get to his feet again and get into position and try to cover the net. Then he was up. Moore's back was to him. He felt stunned but he was doing things by instinct. He sped to the front of the net just as the pass came out. Moore had his stick poised to deflect it when Bill hit him from the side again. It was less of a body check than a covering, enveloping movement, accompanied by a good, stiff shoulder jolt. Bill was like a fighter who had been knocked a little groggy by a good blow. He was trying to gain time to recover his sense. He carried Moore into the back boards and pinned him there, staring vacantly through the glass at the startled faces of some reporters coming in who had seen all this.

Then Moore saw who had checked him. He uttered a sharp epithet and swung his elbow. It missed. Moore was squirming around, obviously ready to fight. Wares did blow the whistle that time. He came up grinning. "Okay, you two," he said. "Knock it off."

CHAPTER 6 ■

"What happened between you and Benny yesterday?" Pam Moore asked him the next day. She had worked now two afternoons in a row. They were in the coffee shop off the hotel lobby. It was late afternoon. Most of the other players had gone to play golf. Bill never had played golf. To tell the truth, today he'd wished he was a golfer. He found that as the week wore on he was getting jumpy about what was going to happen at the end of the week, when the first cuts would be made. He didn't want to be one of them and yet every day he felt that no matter what he did, how could they keep a player with so little experience? He forgot the worry in practice – went out there and rushed and hit and tried to break up plays – but after a workout was over, he missed someone telling him how he was doing. Now the last thing he wanted to talk about was Benny Moore – especially with Benny Moore's sister. And yet she had asked.

He shrugged and tried to change the subject. "There wasn't much to it," he said. "Have a hamburger?" She shook her head. He ordered two for himself and a milkshake. "Not even a milkshake?" he said to her earnestly. She smiled and shook her head again.

There weren't many people around at that time of day. They had the place almost to themselves. She was wearing a green corduroy dress and the green went well with her hair.

"Nothing much to it!" she said, tartly. "There was enough to have all the scouts talking about it last night. I asked Benny. He just about took my head off. So I *know* there's something!"

Bill couldn't suppress a slight chuckle. "He just about took my head off, too," he said. Her face went suddenly pale. He added hastily, "I mean, there was nothing to it! I happened to knock him down on one rush and he happened to knock me down on another."

She was only partly reassured. "To hear the scouts talk about it, it was like a big feud or something." She pushed her straw around in the cracked ice of her half-gone Coke. "I get worried about my brother sometimes. I've always been afraid he'd hurt somebody." It was almost as if she was talking to herself. "He and my granddad, they used to fight something awful. But Granddad was too old, I guess."

There were a lot of things Bill would have liked to ask. He didn't. One thing, anyway, she apparently hadn't heard anything about today's scrimmage. Because the feud had gone right on. Maybe she wouldn't.

But she did, of course. She could read. By the next day, whoever read the sports pages knew all there was to know about the high school kid named Bill Spunska, and his feud with Bad Benny Moore.

Bill started to find out what it was like to live in a goldfish bowl when the six-thirty a.m. call came the next morning. The voice of the night man on the desk usually said nothing but, "Good morning. Six-thirty." This morning he asked, "Is that Mr. Spunska or Mr. Merrill?"

Bill said sleepily, "Spunska."

"There's a big story about you and Benny Moore in the paper this morning," the man said. "Thought you would like to know."

In the other bed as Bill hung up, Tim Merrill rolled off his side onto his back. He had his hands behind his head. Since morning calls were such routine things, he had noticed the difference this time. "What was that?" he asked.

Bill said, "He said there was something in the paper this morning about Benny Moore and me."

There was a shadow of a smile on Merrill's face. "How's your head this morning?"

Bill gingerly felt the place just behind his right ear up high where he had hit his head on the protective glass. He'd made the mistake of trying to go between Moore and the boards. Moore had taken him low with his leg and hip and high with his elbow and stick. The force of the impact plus Bill's own forward motion had made it quite a collision. Bill had seen a big, flashing light before his eyes as he went down. He had been up again immediately, but really groggy. The lump was still tender.

Merrill swung his legs out of bed and headed for the shower. Because of his seniority it was an understood thing that he got first crack at the shower. "How did you and Moore get started on this bumping?"

Bill told him about the first night in the room. "The funny thing was I think he wanted to see you and talk to you," Bill said. He paused for a moment. The shower water was running. Before hitting his head yesterday, he'd encountered Moore two or three times in good solid body checks. Anybody keeping score would have had to declare the earlier collisions a draw. But the whole business bothered Bill. He felt an extra tingling of tension when he had the puck and was coming in on Moore or Moore had the puck or was a part of an attack heading his way. He wondered how much of this was the actual contact they'd had so far, and how much was his awareness of Moore's reputation. It was something one couldn't ignore when a player had a reputation for losing his temper, swinging his stick, and things like that.

He knew there wouldn't be much more said about it by Merrill. Even the little bit there had been was rare in the camp atmosphere. They kidded one another, told jokes on one another, but there was very little that could be termed internal gossip. But Bill was curious about what was in the paper.

Merrill came out of the shower. Bill stepped in. The hot water hit him hard. He'd never been much for cold showers and couldn't see that they did anybody any good. He was wide awake to start with and didn't need the shock of cold water to help him along.

When Bill came out of the shower and grabbed his underwear and started dressing, Merrill was brushing his hair in front of the mirror. "I think you've played this Moore thing pretty well so far," he said, looking at his hair, not at Bill. "The only way it could hurt you would be if you backed down or lost your temper. It's sometimes pretty difficult to go along that thin line – being tough enough to get respect, but not so tough that you hurt somebody."

He left it that way. No big exhortation or rigmarole but just a flat statement. Bill could read all the rest into it. Hockey was like a lot of other things in life. Tim was telling him that in hockey you had to have backbone to take it as well as hand it out. Bill got the message.

Downstairs, he bought a paper. It was funny; some of the other amateur tryout guys grumbled about the $200 a week that the club gave them in training camp. To Bill it seemed a fortune. Transportation to camp provided, room and meals provided, nothing to spend it on except the odd movie or maybe a little extra food. It made Bill feel quite affluent to lay out twenty-five cents for a newspaper.

Actually, he needn't have bothered. When he and Merrill and some of the others arrived at the breakfast table, McGarry had struck a pose at the front of the room by the big tureen of scrambled eggs. He had the paper open at the sports page. Moore wasn't in the breakfast room yet. Bill was glad of that. McGarry was reading the story with gestures. Everybody was laughing and throwing in their comments. If Moore had been there, too, Bill felt that there couldn't have been this comic atmosphere about the reading McGarry was giving. Moore would have seen to that.

"Here is the young lion, now," McGarry proclaimed when he saw Bill. "I didn't expect to see you this morning, young fellow, after I read in the paper, where it says right here," he searched through the story, " '. . . and the developing feud came to a head in yesterday's afternoon workout when Moore charged half across the rink to board Spunska, smashing him into the glass with a crash that could be heard in Lindsay, Ontario. Spunska dropped to the ice as if he had been hit over the head with an axe, and appeared groggy when he got to his feet. However, in a minute or two he was all right again. There was no further clash between the young fellow from Winnipeg and Bad Benny for the rest of the workout.' "

McGarry went on reading: " 'Observers at the camp are wondering if coach Pokesy Wares is letting this thing go too far. For one thing, a great deal of importance will be placed on the way Moore acts at training camp. Last year's suspension still is hanging over him. If he gets into any trouble through rough play with his own potential teammates, it's unlikely that anybody in the NHL will take a chance on him. There have been cases in the past . . .' " But at that point he was drowned out by cries of, "Shut up, McGarry, and start eating." Which he did.

Moore came in a little later. He had a paper. Bill read his silently from where McGarry had stopped:

. . . cases in the past where real good hockey players have been dropped out of the big-time simply because they didn't have the character and good sense to take part in the game at its highest level – even though their natural ability might have been greater than some of the ones that did stick around. Moore is more or less on probation in this camp.

Some of you think that if he were going to take on anybody, he would do himself more good by taking on one of the really established Leafs rather than a boy straight out of high school. But anybody who thinks that just hasn't seen Spunska. When he picks up the puck and starts flying down the ice, there's no more formidable figure in hockey anywhere. It certainly isn't a case of a bully and a young rookie.

If you want a prediction, it's this: One of these days, one of these players is going to get cut for a few stitches and then Wares will call a halt. All he has to do is switch either Moore or Spunska to another training shift. The matter would be suspended there.

Bill also read the first part of the story. It said that this weekend, according to Coach Wares, twelve players would be cut from the camp. The writer did not undertake to guess which ones would be kept around for another week. Bill scanned that part quickly to see if any names were mentioned. None was. "The ones who will be released include some players who still have a year or so of junior left, and others who despite good reputations just haven't shown much at this camp," the story read. Bill wondered, is that good or bad for me? He didn't know.

As Bill was leaving the room, Moore was going out, too. It would have been easy not to say hello. Moore and Bill had several other players between them. But Moore caught Bill's eye and grinned. "How's the head?" he asked.

Bill wished he could think of something bright to say. He couldn't. He grinned back, "Fine," he said. "Good," Moore said and kept on going. Times like that, Bill almost liked him. But he had to deal with the other Moore, too, the on-ice Moore, rough and rebellious and giving no quarter. It wouldn't do to forget that other Moore.

On the way to the rink, Bill was walking with Jiggs Maniscola and Jim Butt. Bill didn't think Butt had said three words a day since the incident of coming without his skates. That crack of Deyell's – "Didn't you think you might need skates to make this hockey team?" – had been repeated through all the other shifts and dressing rooms and among the scouts in the lobby by now. Butt was a loping, clumsy farm boy until he got on those skates. Then, Bill thought, Butt was more effective than any other forward in camp outside of the Leafs. He'd match Butt against some of them, too. Now Butt was walking along as silent at usual.

But Maniscola spoke to Bill. "You know why Moore is sore at you?"

Bill shook his head. They were walking under some big maples, with the leaves just beginning to turn. It was another still, crisp September day without a cloud in the sky. It seemed too nice a day to worry about small things. "Well, one thing – Moore doesn't really need a reason," Maniscola said. "Those few games he played with the Leafs, he cut that Henry Cannon from Montreal for about ten stitches with the blade of his stick in the corner. I think it was accidental, but once Moore does a thing he seems to think he's got to justify it. They'd gone into the corner together after the puck and Cannon got tripped or something and sort of fell back against Moore and caught him with an elbow and then Moore's stick came up and hit him on the forehead. So it's an accident! But when I skated over there, they were getting up, and Moore was saying to Cannon, 'Next time I'll take your head off.' "

They walked along for another half block. The rink was in sight. "But the big thing," Maniscola said, "is you made Moore look bad on that one play right at the beginning, first scrimmage."

"But anyone can look bad on one play!" Bill said. "I mean, Annie Oakley went around me the first time he came in on me so fast that it took me about twenty seconds to get my legs untied, but . . ." here he gave a rueful grin, "that kind of thing is happening to me all the time."

Maniscola said, "There's no use talking about what *you* would have done in the same situation, Spunska. We're talking about Moore. That's a different thing altogether. He would have been sore at anybody who made him look bad. The next time that guy came in on him with the puck, Moore would have got a piece of him or died in the attempt. But to have an eighteen-year-old kid straight from high school, especially one he'd kidded, knock him flat and get away a good shot on goal – why, the kind of guy Benny Moore is, that's the unforgivable!"

The silent Butt made one of his rare remarks as they waited for the light just a hundred yards from the entrance to the rink. "He needs a friend," Butt said.

The light changed. Maniscola and Bill both took a startled look at Butt as they started across the street.

CHAPTER 7 ▬

Bill hung around the lobby after dinner, that Friday night. He knew from the papers a cut-down meeting was on: coaches and scouts. But maybe it wouldn't take long. Maybe Mr. Jackson would come down and let him know who was going to be around next week. He bought a magazine and read, or tried to read. In his mind he kept imagining a small headline, in a Winnipeg paper: SPUNSKA CUT BY LEAFS. But what did he expect? Just because he wanted to stay didn't mean he deserved to stay. Yet he couldn't get out of his head the idea that he *did* deserve to stay. Over and over again, he went through the list. He tried to do it coldly, grading the others as if they had nothing to do with him at all. And every time, he wound up being in the first eight. So were Moore, Givens, Butt. . . . He put Butt first on every list he made. If they only cut ten tonight, he should stick. . . .

His feet hit the tiled floor of the lobby with a crash.

"You nervous or something?" the night desk clerk asked coldly.

"I guess so," Bill said. He wished Pam was around tonight. He thought of asking the desk clerk what room she had. . . . Maybe she'd like a Coke or something. Darn it! Players in small groups strolled in and out of the lobby. Some of them smiled at him and some did not. The three regular sportswriters came out, the tall one talking and the other two listening. Jim Butt came along and sat down.

"Hear the latest?" he asked.

"No what?" Bill asked. He glanced automatically toward the place by the elevator where the notices usually were posted.

Butt grinned. "Not that!" he said. "Nothing official."

Bill slumped deeply in the chesterfield. "What then?"

"Did you know that Adam and Eve were once Leaf supporters?"

For a second or two Bill didn't get it. When he did, he let out such a snort of laughter that three scouts emerged from behind a potted palm to see what all the noise was about. Jim told them, too.

In the general laughter, Bill felt better. The elevator doors opened and Pamela Moore stepped out. A few minutes earlier, Bill had been in such a sombre mood that he might not have done more than say hello and let her go on by. But now as she passed, seeming in quite a hurry, he scrambled to his feet and towered over her. Butt got up, too. Otto Tihane was going by. "A rose between two thorns," he said.

"Are you going anywhere we could walk with you?" Bill asked. He blurted it out, including Jim, too. "Not me!" Jim said hastily. "That walking back and forth from the rink has just about done me!"

Pam's eyes looked startled and troubled. She hesitated before giving an answer.

"I'm sitting around here going nuts waiting for somebody to come and tell me to pack up and head back to Winnipeg," Bill said. "Even if I only got out and walked, I wouldn't be waiting for that tap on the shoulder." He shuddered as if scared to death. It wasn't all acting.

Pam said, "Thanks all the same, but . . ."

"But the lady's going to meet another guy," Butt said.

"That's all right!" Bill started to say. "I mean, it's all right with me. . . ." He hadn't really stopped to think of that particular matter before. But heck, they just talked over the counter sometimes. It was just casual. . . . What could Pam have against him going with her, even to meet another fellow?

"I think I'd better go alone," she said, with a sudden laugh. "I'm going to meet another fellow all right – Benny!" She turned and smiled up at Bill. *"Now* can you see?"

Bill grinned. "It's just when one of us has the puck I bother him," he said. "But maybe you're right." All the same, he wondered, why didn't Benny come here? He'd been at supper – or had he? Bill hadn't seen him, come to think of it. The sister stuff was all very well, but a girl didn't want to be walking around the streets alone at night. "Do you have far to go?" he asked.

She hesitated again. "No," she said uncertainly. "Not far." But before more could be said, she turned and left, her high heels clicking on the tiles.

"Pretty girl," Jim said, as they watched her go.

"Sure is," Bill said.

"Show?" Butt said.

"Guess so," Bill said.

When they returned two and half hours later, there was still no word. No sign by the elevator to indicate who had been cut. "No nothing!" Butt said.

"Maybe they won't put it up," Bill said. "Maybe they'll just call the players in and tell them. Maybe Mr. Jackson does it."

Butt was scratching his long, freckled nose. The clock above the desk said ten-fifteen. "It's about bedtime," he said.

Tomorrow was Saturday. An exhibition game was scheduled between Leafs and Chicago in St. Catharines for Saturday night. So the schedule of morning workouts had been changed; early shift at nine instead of eight, second shift at ten, lunch, and then the bus to St. Catharines leaving in mid-afternoon. But the curfew tonight was the same as usual, eleven. Players returning from various movies were streaming back through the lobby now, picking up papers or magazines, ribbing one another. Tim Merrill stopped beside Jim and Bill. Tim had an unerring eye. "I suppose you two are waiting around to see if the cuts are posted, eh?"

Bill nodded, looking at him, hoping to hear something reassuring.

"No use," Tim said. "They always put 'em up in the morning. It'll be after the workout tomorrow. Not a chance in the world of you finding out now. May as well come up to bed."

When Bill was going to bed a little later, he said his prayers, as usual. He didn't try to put his hopes into words, but he thought of it. He thought of the week to come – if he could stick! If he could stick for next week, maybe he could survive for the week after that, too! And then he thought of the kids who wouldn't make it. He wondered if they all were wondering as he was – trying not to show it, but wondering every second.

His light was out. The first time he had prayed while Tim was in the room, Tim had looked at him a little startled. From then on, it was taken for granted. Now Tim turned out his light, too, and Bill fixed the blinds. As he was doing so, there was a screech of tires out in front. He looked down. The clock in front of the hotel showed one minute to eleven. A taxi had come to a jumping halt in front of the hotel. Benny Moore was getting out. Quickly he paid the driver and raced into the hotel.

Bill thought of mentioning it to Tim but didn't. Anything he said about Benny Moore would sound like part of their feud. . . . But where was Pam? She'd been going to meet Benny, she'd said. Of course, Bill had been at that show – maybe she'd come back when he was away. He climbed between the sheets. He lay there for a while on his back thinking of her. Where had Benny been that he had to come rushing up in a cab with one minute to go? Wouldn't you think a guy under the gun like that would be more careful? He wondered if Pam really was back. There was no way he could find out now, after curfew.

His last thought was, will I be cut? He dreamed he was, and had to walk all the way back to Winnipeg.

CHAPTER 8

Squib Jackson had walked through the open door of Pokesy Wares's corner suite on the second floor of the hotel earlier on that Friday night, about seven. Wares had looked up. "Late, as usual, you old crook!" he said. "What've you been doing – winning all the spending money back from those rookies at cribbage?"

"Why, you bald-headed so-and-so!" Squib said. "Just because you insist on donating your money every time somebody gets you sitting at a table doesn't mean . . ."

"Meeting is called to order!" the coach said hastily. Anyone who didn't know these two would think they were deadly enemies. Jackson had signed Wares many years before as a player for the Leafs, but after not making the grade at his first camp, he had decided coaching was the way he could stay in the game he loved. Jackson always grinned to himself when he heard people say cynical things about Pokesy Wares. He acted tough. He was tough. But he was still as much in love with hockey as any dewy-eyed kid.

"Hi," Squib said in a general greeting to the other three in the room. They sat together at workouts every day, so no elaborate greeting was necessary. Hub Wiley and Percy Simpson were from St. Catharines. Wiley was a dapper fat man who managed the team there, Leafs' farm. Percy did the coaching. Years before goalie masks were standard, he'd been a good goalie, but one night he'd lost sight of a puck in flight. A shot puck travels ninety to one hundred miles an hour. This one hit him in the right eye. He had lost so much vision that he'd never played goal again. Percy had black hair that was going grey and he wore an eye patch. The fourth chair was filled by King Casey, assistant coach and manager to Wares. King had been in the game since he got out of rompers – player, referee, coach, manager, and general Ottawa Valley Irishman, as he said himself.

The room had broadloom to the walls. The dusk outside was deepening but the blinds were not drawn. A tray of coffee cups and some thermos jugs sat on top of the TV set.

Each man had a clipboard in his hand. The coach had a card table set up in front of him with lists of names on several sheets of paper. Squib was still standing. "Sit down, Squib!" the coach said. "Start thinking. We've got to cut a bunch of these kids."

Squib sat. "Well, I don't think you've got to cut so many," he said mildly.

Wares threw down his pencil. "You're always the same, Jackson!" he said. "If you had your way we'd have sixty kids here right up until about fifteen minutes before we're supposed to play our opening game! We've got to start cutting down! Now, I want to get ten or twelve kids out of this camp by tomorrow night. Let's just see how we can do it without hurting ourselves."

The coach passed Squib copies of the lists he had in front of him. On List One were the names of all the Leaf players, on List Two the names of all the minor pro players. List Three contained the names of professionals who had come into the organization during the summer either by draft or by returning from being loaned to clubs in other leagues. If they didn't make St. Catharines or the Leafs, they would be released or placed elsewhere again this winter. The fourth list was of amateurs.

"Now, the way I look at it," Wares said, "we can start with List Three. Decide which of these we can do without. This might get some guys off our necks who are hanging around the camp now." He was referring to representatives of independent minor league pro teams who haunted the various NHL camps trying to pick up players. "I'll read off the names of guys I think we can get rid of. If there are any objections, let me know." He looked at Wiley and Simpson. "Especially if I read off anybody you want. But if I don't want them and you don't want them, let's see if we can find somebody who does."

He read off the names slowly. Squib knew every man. There was a bit of a twinge every time a name was called and nobody objected to his being shipped elsewhere, if a taker could be found. Squib had talked to all these young men at one time or another. He knew all their hopes and their ambitions. It wasn't his fault, nor theirs perhaps, that they weren't good enough to play hockey in the kind of company they wanted to play in. That didn't make the job of cutting them any easier.

The coach read off six names. There wasn't a word from the St. Catharines pair. At the end, the St. Catherines coach read off a couple of other names and said he wasn't interested in them either.

"Maybe you're not interested in them," King Casey said with a chuckle. "But we happen to know a couple of guys from other clubs right now who *are* interested in both those. We'll just keep them around and hope they'll look so good in the next couple of days that we can trade them for something we do want."

Squib thought, sometimes we get a little callous. In a meeting like this, they're just names. We forget what it means to some of them to be dropped or shipped out somewhere else. But this was part of the game, and the player knew that. He could always quit if he didn't like what was happening to him. Some of these fringe minor league pros could go back home and within a matter of weeks get a job, play for some local team and try to forget that they ever had higher ambitions. Many did that. Others suffered a little. But there were good players in the National Hockey League who had been shunted around the minors a lot – until they got the experience and skill that made them valuable in the big-time.

"We might want to do some shuffling back and forth between the Leafs and St. Catharines in the next week or so," Wares said, thoughtfully, waving his hands at a cloud of cigarette smoke set up by Wiley. Wares didn't smoke. "Some of those guys of mine are acting as if they've got the job made! I'd like to shake some of them up a little. I'll send you a couple of forwards and maybe a defenceman for that exhibition game you've got on Monday night in Kitchener. I'll maybe pick up a couple of yours to take with us to Niagara Falls. Okay?" He looked at Percy Simpson.

"Okay," said Simpson.

There was a pause. Squib looked over the list of amateurs that he knew would be the next order of business. This was where he had to dig in his heels and fight. There was always a tendency in the professional teams to try to cut down to size fast so that training could proceed in a more orderly fashion. Squib's conviction was that this was the wrong way to go about it. A lot of young players needed more than a week to show what they had.

"Now the young ones," Pokesy said. "Who goes back on the bus for home?"

There was a pause before he went on. "How do you guys think Moore has been doing?" he asked.

The two from St. Catharines came alive fast. "He looks good to us," they said. "I think we should turn him pro."

"I don't want to turn him pro until we find out about this suspension!" Wares said. "Coffee, Squib? Get me some too, will you?" Squib didn't stop listening as he poured from the thermos jugs. "I mean," Wares said, "if he's going to be suspended longer than the end of this month he isn't going to be any good for anything until they spring him."

"Couldn't you give the league president a call on an unofficial basis?" King Casey asked, in his gravelly voice. "I mean, tell him the kid has a good chance but if we have to wait until the end of September to know whether he's available we might just have to make some other arrangements."

"Well, I could try that," Wares said. "You think he's going that well?"

Wiley answered that. "It's not the way he's going so much as the way he looks out there!" he said. "Darn it, that kid's got a lot of colour! I can sure imagine our crowds going for him!"

Squib looked at Wiley rather sourly. "I know you've got to sell tickets," he said. "But this kid is a real risk. He isn't going to do you any good at the gate in the long run if he hauls off and hits some referee over the head with his hockey stick and gets barred for life! I don't think he's showed yet that he's got the attitude to make a career in this organization."

Simpson argued heatedly, "Look! There are guys around this camp right now from two or three other clubs in our league that are dying to get their hands on Moore. How would I explain it to our fans and sportswriters if we let him get away? He'd come in and play against us and not only murder us but look twice as interesting as any guy we've got doing it!"

Squib wouldn't be stirred. "I still don't think he's ready, mentally," he said doggedly. "To be with us, he's got to behave."

The Leaf coach had been listening. "Let's give Moore another week. I think he's a good enough hockey player to be a pro. I also agree with Squib – whether he should be a pro with our organization is another thing."

Wiley was annoyed. "You guys are pretty pious about what's good enough to play in the Leaf organization, aren't you? Of course, you don't have to sell tickets – your rink is always full."

"We are choosy," Wares said cheerfully. "And sometimes we've been wrong. Some guys we let get away we paid plenty to get back later."

King Casey interrupted. "And some have been foul balls from the word go and we saved ourselves nothing but trouble by cutting them loose. Don't forget that!"

"That Moore!" Squib said. "I wish I knew what made that kid tick." He shook his head. "A little while ago I ran into him in the lobby, headed out some place. He was broke, said he couldn't get along on two hundred a week. Bummed more. I gave him next week's and told him that this was all there was and he better get along on it. Then I went into the dining room and ran into Spunska and Butt. Just for fun I asked how much they had left."

"So?" King asked.

"Spunska, a hundred and eighteen, the other kid, a hundred and twenty."

Everybody laughed. Then Wares said, "You

got a lot of nerve giving money to Moore before we even decide who's going to be cut, haven't you?"

Squib looked shocked. "You're not planning on cutting Moore!"

As soon as he said it, he realized that not many people told the Leaf coach what he could or could not do about his hockey players. To his relief, Wares laughed. "You're right. But let's take them in order, starting at the top of the list. I want to hear what each one of you has to say about these kids."

As the name of each of the amateurs was read, the coaches and scouts would comment.

Wares read, "Maniscola."

Simpson: "If he could just shoot a little better, we could use him."

Wiley: "I think maybe we can use him anyway. He seems ready to me."

King Casey: "The kid will be with the Leafs within two years."

Squib: "He's showed me a lot of improvement. He's twice the skater he was last year."

Maniscola's name was left on the list. Some other players weren't so lucky. One of these was Garth Givens.

Simpson: "I think another year of junior would do him a lot of good. That big looping skating style seems to have him mesmerized. He never goes straight in one direction. He's always got to make a bunch of circles to get there."

Casey: "He reminds me of a guy we used to have up in Ottawa. One night they left the door of the rink open and he skated about two miles down the Rideau Canal before he realized that nobody was feeding him any passes."

Squib: "He's got a lot of natural talent. Put him back in junior for a year and tell him why. I think he's bright enough to develop."

Wares: "I'd go for that."

When they came to Jim Butt, there was an argument. Squib started it. "Here's a kid could turn pro right away, if he was going to get the right kind of coaching."

Simpson: "I don't think we could use him, do you? He's too skinny to last in the rough going we get down there."

Wares: "I think you're underestimating that kid, Percy. Ever see the way he skates? If there was ever a kid who reminds me of Gordie Howe, he's the one. Built like him, too. Got a disposition like him. He wouldn't harm a fly off the ice. On the ice nobody gets away with much, with him. He's got another year of junior, too, hasn't he?"

Squib Jackson: "Yeah. But we got a problem with him. He's been very bright all the way through high school. He's had several offers of scholarships from U.S. universities. I don't know that he'd turn pro with us even if we offered him the chance. But I am pretty sure that if we don't offer him the chance he's going to sign with one of those colleges and probably be gone for four years."

The Leaf coach said, "He doesn't look that bright."

Squib said, "You should see the farm he comes from. You can stand right in the middle of it – the country's as flat as this table – and you can't see the edges of the farm in any direction, it's so big. That kid just sits on a tractor all day out there and thinks, as far as I can make out. In the spring time he even studies on the tractor. He comes from quite a family. They went out there about eighty years ago and homesteaded and they've done nothing but buy more land ever since. Not one of them ever went to anything but an agricultural college, but this kid doesn't want to be a farmer."

"What does he want to be?" Wares asked.

Squib said, "I've talked to the kid a hundred times and I still don't know. He doesn't say much; I always wind up realizing that I've done all the talking. I think he just wants to get off that big farm and see if he can't get part of the Butt family going in some other direction. He's quite happy to leave the farm to some of his brothers."

There was a little pause, and then Squib added, "That's one way I got him to come here. I told him that if he played pro hockey for a few years he'd get into the big cities and maybe he'd get a better idea of what he wanted to do in life."

Wares let off steam suddenly. "I wish just once I'd come to camp with a pile of hockey players who wanted to do nothing but play hockey!" he said. "These guys with ambitions to do anything but play hockey give me a great big pain! Don't they know the good Lord only gives them one real talent each? If a guy's good enough at hockey to get to our camp he should do his level best to make it to the Leafs and if he doesn't make it he should be goldarn sorry for himself. That's the time when he should start thinking of doing something else with his life! College for a kid like that - phooey!"

Jackson said smoothly, "May I pass on those views about higher education to the Toronto newspapers?"

Wares said, "You do, and I'll keep you on those open-air rinks in Saskatchewan from December to March."

An hour had passed. Then an hour and a half. Finally they got to Spunska.

Wares said, "I'm not convinced that we should keep this kid another week."

Squib said nothing. He was sure Pokesy was

kidding, and he waited for the comments of the others.

King: "He's going to be a good one."

Simpson: "He's sure green! The way he lunges out from the blueline at puck carriers sometimes. There are some guys in the NHL and the AHL, too, who would just see him do that once and then they'd know every time how they were going to get in and get a shot on goal."

Squib: "They'd get around him just once, and then he'd figure out what he'd done wrong and he wouldn't do it again. He's smart."

Pokesy: "I know you're awfully high on this kid."

Squib: "I wouldn't have brought anybody straight from a high school league that I didn't think was exceptional."

Wiley: "What's with this feud between Spunska and Moore? I know that officially it just started over some words the two kids had the first night they were in here. But Spunska doesn't look like a kid that would annoy Moore all that much."

Squib: "That's another reason why you should not sign Moore until you look at him a little more. He's the kind of a guy that takes a grudge at somebody and then tries to nail him every time he goes onto the ice! That's all that's happened with this kid, Spunska. Spunska's big and green and he got Moore mad at him. Moore thought he was going to show Spunska up. The first time he got on the ice, Spunska showed Moore up instead. I've watched this Moore, before. He won't forgive Spunska until something big happens and he's convinced that he's paid off Spunska in full. Sometimes I think we should have a psychiatrist in camp."

Wares exploded. "Never mind Moore! We're talking about Spunska, aren't we?"

The four men nodded.

Wares glanced back over the list of amateurs. "Well, we've cut eight guys off this list. I want twelve off. I'll think about it a little more. Let you know tomorrow."

Squib said mildly, "You're going to be pretty busy tomorrow." He had the feeling that the coach had pretty well made up his mind. He couldn't figure out any reason for the delay. He felt a responsibility to the new kids especially. The pros were different. Most of them were going to be in this camp or some camp; they were older and could look after themselves.

"Maybe I'll see you later tonight," Wares said. "King and I have some phone calls to make before I can make up my mind." Squib knew then that a trade might be in the wind that would change the team's requirements. That was the only reason for delay. "Okay," he said. "I'm going out with some of the scouts tonight, but I should be back around eleven or so. A little later, maybe."

Wares said, "Call me at eleven. I'll have an answer by then."

CHAPTER 9 ▬

In the morning, Bill came wide awake before the phone rang. Tim was still asleep. Bill tossed a bit in bed, tiptoed to the window and looked out at the quiet street, wondering what would happen in the next day or so. There would be a rearrangement of rooms. He'd been told this would happen after the first cut – the Leafs would begin rooming together, so would the St. Catharines players, and the rookies who were left would be mixed in among them. He looked across to the corner where his bag was. His apprehension and excitement were such that he couldn't keep still.

He walked quietly to the bathroom, closed the door, and turned on the shower. As the hot water splashed over him he thought again of Benny Moore coming in last night just in time to beat the curfew. Then the matter of his own survival took over again. He just couldn't get it out of his mind.

When he cautiously opened the bathroom

door a few minutes later, Tim was awake, wearing a big grin. "I hope you stick, kid," he said. That was all, but it helped to know that somebody else knew what he was thinking, too.

As early as Bill was, Jim Butt and Garth Givens had beaten him to the lobby. They were first into the breakfast room – so early that the middle-aged and motherly types behind the food table glanced at the clock in surprise. "You're early," one of them called. "But we are, too. Help yourself."

While they ate, they talked in subdued tones. Once Butt laughed, "We must be the three least confident guys in hockey right now."

The other two smiled at him wanly.

But then they almost lost their appetites. Pokesy Wares came and went to a corner table where he always ate. There hadn't been any notice posted by the elevator when they came down. Givens got up, excused himself, went out and came back a minute later. He sat down. "Nothing there yet," he said.

Then Squib Jackson, arriving, called to them jovially and went on to the coach's table. The two men from St. Catharines came in and went over there, too. And King Casey. They talked in low voices. "I wish that table was wired for sound," Bill said miserably.

At the table they were watching so closely,

Squib said to the Leafs' coach, "I couldn't get you last night."

"I was out," Pokesy said. "Guess where?"

"We don't guess so good in the mornings," King said.

"I had a call just after eleven," Wares said. "The police. Of all the stupid things – you know what Moore did last night?"

They all sat in silence and looked at him.

"He got into a fight at a swimming pool!" Wares said. "Not a poolroom, or a bootlegger's, or anything like that – at a pool! Some young guys said Moore had made some offensive remarks in front of some girls there. I don't know what happened from then on. Won't until I talk to Moore. But the other guy got pushed around a little. The last thing we want around this camp is that kind of trouble. But I'll give that cop a lot of credit. He said they couldn't be absolutely sure that it was Moore's fault. No charges or anything, but he wanted me to come down to the police station and see this other kid." Pokesy jabbed viciously at a piece of sausage, chewed, and then said, "Never mind that right now. I'm only going to cut the eight we decided on last night. That leaves a lot more to cut next week. But with all those exhibition games we have coming up for both clubs, we'll be able to work in a few extra somewhere between the two camps we split into now." He meant the Leafs and St. Catharines camps.

Simpson said, "Who you going to take with Leafs?"

"How many defencemen have we got between the two camps?" Wares said as he counted through the lists with his pencil. "Fourteen. Seven each. I'll take mostly Leafs and one of those kids, Moore or Spunska, for a game or two. Take your pick, which one do you want?"

"Moore!" Wiley said instantly.

"King, you see if we can get him cleared for exhibitions with St. Catharines." Wares sighed. "Wouldn't this be great, if he's in another jam?"

Simpson said, "We have radio, TV, and newspaper people coming for our exhibitions next week. If they see Moore once, they're going to be awfully annoyed if we don't have him there on the ice when we open the season in October."

Wares said, "You can take him for these exhibitions. But I think one of you guys had better have a talk with him right away. Maybe you, too, Squib. I'll see him right after he comes off the ice this morning. You guys wait until he gets back here. We've got to impress on him that the way he acts in the next little while is going to determine whether we keep him in this outfit at all."

"There's nothing else we can do, is there?" Simpson said. "I mean, we've got to lay it right on the line. Either he behaves, or else."

"Go to it," the coach said.

As they were rising to go, Pokesy said, "Squib – one more thing. These two kids, Moore and Spunska. I think it's gone far enough."

Squib was surprised. The coach had a reputation for letting squabbles within the club work themselves out – as long as they weren't causing the rest of the players any trouble. "What are you going to do about it?" he asked, a little sarcastically. "Tell them to stop body-checking?"

Pokesy looked at him with that quizzical smile that meant he'd been saving something and was about to spring it. "There's got to be some shifting around in rooms when we send these others home," he said. "I'm going to move Spunska and Moore in together. Same room."

Wiley exclaimed, "For gosh sakes, Pokesy, why? I mean, if we're trying to keep that Moore kid straight, isn't he better with an older guy who'll keep an eye on him?"

Wares said, "Do you want to have to keep an eye on him every second he's not playing, if you get him? He's got to sink or swim. If he can't room with a kid like Spunska and keep his nose clean, we're going to get rid of him." To the protests of the men from St. Catharines he said,

"We won't give him away – and you'll probably get whatever we get in trade for him, so quit crying!"

"I'm not so worried about Moore," Squib said. "But what about Spunska?" He glared at Wares. "How would you like to be in his place, getting told that Benny Moore was your new roommate?"

Wares laughed. "I wouldn't," he said.

A few minutes later, Tim Merrill, Jim Butt, and Bill came out of the elevator on their way to the rink. Givens had gone on. Squib was waiting for the elevator. "Better walk fast, men," he said.

The two rookies nodded dumbly. But Tim said, "Who's been cut, Squib? Can't you see those hang-dog looks? These fellows just can't wait to go back home, Squib! Can't you put them out of their misery?"

The little scout shook his head emphatically. "Not me!" he said. "You know how Pokesy is about running this club himself! Boy, you wouldn't catch me making any announcements he's supposed to make!"

"We know that!" Bill said. "We weren't really waiting to ask you. We were just . . ."

". . . waiting to ask you!" Jim Butt said with a laugh.

The elevator left. Squib let it go. He said earnestly, "You can see my position. I mean, the coach hasn't actually shot anybody yet for doing things he's supposed to do himself, but there's always a first time. Sometimes when I hear the things he calls me I think that if there's ever going to be a first time, he'll shoot me! No, sir, I couldn't take a chance!"

"We really do understand," Bill said. He was grinning a bit now.

"You'll know later. I suppose you'll go along to watch the game in St. Catharines, if there's room on the bus? Might see you then. I'm just sorry I can't tell you anything that will put you out of your misery right now, about being cut, I mean. But I can't."

Bill wondered why he kept saying this, while they kept saying they understood. But now he noticed a small light in Mr. Jackson's eyes. The little scout reached inside his jacket for a wallet. Took it out. Opened it. All this time, he was saying, "Can't tell you a thing! Not a thing!" Then he handed ten twenties to Bill and the same to Jim. "Can't tell you a thing," he said. "But I guess there's no reason why I shouldn't give you next week's pocket money – now that you're standing right here. Save me time later."

Tim Merrill had been watching and listening with a big grin on his long, lantern-jawed face. "I told you he wouldn't let you know," he said.

"If you let this out before Pokesy does," Squib said fiercely, "I'll fry you both!"

The relief Bill felt came over him like a wave, making him feel taller, stronger, handsomer, a better hockey player, older, smarter, infinitely more sure of himself. "Thanks!" he said. But his voice hadn't improved any. He just about strangled on the one word, it was pitched so high. "Thanks!" he said again, more normally.

It was all Tim Merrill could do to keep up in the walk to the rink. "Hey, you two," he kept on saying, all the way, "wait for me!"

CHAPTER 10 ▬

They barged into the dressing room with only fifteen minutes to go. The few minutes they'd spent talking to Squib Jackson had cut it pretty fine. Bobby Deyell let them know about it. But they all managed to make it to the ice in lots of time.

There hadn't ever been a practice like that one, for Bill. The load he'd been carrying the last couple of days was gone – until next weekend and the next cuts anyway, he thought, smiling wryly. He felt as light as a bird. The players skated circuits of the rink to get warmed up. Bill went around like a bull moose, passing people, yelling at the ones he knew best, even letting out an Indian yell once in a while. Tim Merrill came up beside him once and said, "Better cool off. Anybody sees you acting like this, they'll *know* you know." Bill slowed down a little, but slowing down was tough on a morning like this.

The players all carried their sticks. Some skated alone and some in groups. Sometimes a man would stop and say a few words to another and skate with him for half the length of the rink and then spurt on or fall back. Some players skated backwards. Some skated counter-clockwise. Skaters who skate mainly for pleasure get into the habit of going only one way, circling constantly to the left. In this respect Bill had been lucky. The first time he'd put on skates it had been in an attempt to learn how to be a hockey player. He turned to his right as strongly as to his left.

Wares stepped to the ice with his baseball cap and whistle. Blew a blast. They all skated to the middle to get their orders. As Bill got there, McGarry was talking to a group around him. "All right, you Leafs," he called, imitating the coach, "you've got a tough exhibition game tonight against Chicago, so you just go back to the hotel and sleep . . ."

"McGarry," said the inflexible voice of the coach interrupting. "Three times around the rink!"

There was a burst of jeering for McGarry from the other players. "Coach!" wailed McGarry, standing still. "Old pal! My friend! I was just kidding. I was misquoted."

"Five times around the rink," the coach said.

McGarry started out, talking every step. Wares yelled after him, "We'll let you know what to do after that." Then he turned to the others. Bill had learned to smile inwardly at the coach's tough manner. But he had rather expected, too, that the players who'd be playing tonight would get off a little easy this morning. Showed how far a rookie could be wrong.

"The usual workout," the coach said. "I'll give it to you as we go along. And any of you who are going to play tonight and who think you're in such good shape that you don't need this workout – go ahead! Go back to the hotel! Those who go back I will want to see after the game tonight so you can explain fully anything you've done wrong in the game. And if you have done anything wrong, there'll be a two-hour extra workout right here tomorrow morning, for people who miss the one this morning only. Who's leaving?"

Nobody was leaving. Bill thought, nobody really wanted to – even McGarry, now toiling around shouting pitiful pleas every time he came within earshot. This was part of the way the coach worked. He saved his direst threats for eventualities that he knew didn't have a chance of happening. Who would leave a workout now and take a chance that some fancy Dan would go around him tonight and cost him two hours' extra work tomorrow morning? Nobody! And who would want to miss this greatest of all possible practices anyway? Bill was still feeling ten feet tall, just knowing he'd survived this first cut. He felt he could do anything, today!

"Starts and stops!" the coach called. "Get going."

All players gathered at one end of the rink. Wares blew the whistle. Everybody skated as hard as he could until the whistle blew again – then all stopped in a shower of snow thrown up by their skates. This happened four times between one end of the rink and the other. The idea was to get players used to quick starts and stops.

Wares explained this briefly once a day. "In hockey, you're not speed skaters, or river skaters, as some people liked to call them," he said. "By that I mean it doesn't matter a darn how far or how fast you can skate, if you haven't got manoeuvrability. You've got to be able to stop and go in another direction so fast that a man who can't do it as well can't catch you – but you can catch him no matter what he does."

Bill had seen quickly also that stops and starts, besides making the blood pound and the sweat stand out, taught them by competition to start fast and stop fast. After going up and down the ice a couple of times with stops and starts, the slow starters would be well back of the others. Nobody wanted to be last. Bill had been considered a fast starter in the class of hockey he played in. He'd been one of the slowest here, the first time down the ice. The next time he'd been a little better. Even old Buff Koska, who was supposed to be a slow defenceman, had beaten him on those whistles at first. He didn't any more. But Moore did, by a few feet every whistle.

"Line rushes," the coach called.

Forward lines formed up at one end of the rink, three men each to go in on two defencemen at the other end. The lines would work right in until they got a shot on the goal. At that moment, or when a defenceman got possession of the puck, that rush would end and the puck would be fed to another line going in the other direction against another two defencemen. King Casey stood on the sidelines and gave advice in his rasping voice, and sometimes Wares would go over to a player and speak to him.

Then for a few minutes they practised two-on-one rushes – two men carrying the puck and passing it back and forth, coming in on one defenceman. Bill watched closely to see how the others did it, looking for techniques he could pick up. "Don't commit yourself!" Wares would yell. "Keep your body between the puck carrier and the goal and your stick between the puck carrier and the other guy! Then he's got to be good to beat you!"

Then five minutes of the shooting practice

that was known to the sportswriters as "idiot's delight." This consisted of lining up fifteen men across the blueline, each with half a dozen pucks, facing in on goal. At the coach's whistle shooting began. The man at the extreme right of the line would fire, then the man next to him, then the man next to him, and so on across the ice and back – the goalie dancing and leaping to make the save – until all the pucks had been shot. The second round was the really tough part. The man at the extreme right would fire; then the man at the extreme left. Second man at the right and then second man at the left. All this was done as rapidly as the sticks could come down and hit the puck and drive it toward the goal. Johnny Bosfield had to plunge back and forth across the goal mouth under a real rain of rubber. But he bore up well. The only thing he didn't like was high shots. If a shot was below his waist or chest, it wasn't dangerous, because he was thickly padded down there. But high, it could be dangerous, even with the mask. Percy Simpson from St. Catharines, now sitting high in the stands to watch from his one eye, could tell you that. And he hadn't ever worn a mask.

Bill was developing a wrist turn at the end of his shot, a sort of a follow-through, that he had noticed being done by the good shooters. Butt shot this way, too. He apparently did it naturally. In one of his rare moments of communication, he had told Bill that last year was the only year of organized hockey he'd played. Before that he'd been a kid playing with men's teams around the home village in Saskatchewan. The reason no scouts had picked him up and moved him was because he'd been so small – "I only weighed 115 pounds until a year ago," Butt said. "Then I put on forty pounds in a year."

At 8:45, the brief scrimmage began. Bobby Deyell tossed around the white jerseys.

Every morning when this happened, Bill wondered if Wares would change his mind and put him and Moore on the same team. Again this morning, they were opposed to one another, Moore with the Whites, Bill with the Blues. On the first shift of the scrimmage he found himself on defence with Otto Tihane. Moore was at the other end with Buff Koska.

As Bill stood on the blueline with Tihane, waiting for the puck to be dropped, the tough old defenceman turned to him and smiled pleasantly. "Who's going to get the stitches today, you or Moore?"

Bill said, "I hope neither of us."

"Not much chance, the way you've been going for each other," Tihane said.

Actually they got through that scrimmage with no stitches at all. Four collisions. Four times both went down. Then it was nine o'clock and the next shift was waiting.

Moore was right in front of Bill, leaving the ice. The coach was waiting at the gate. "Moore," he said.

Moore said, "Me?"

"Yeah," Wares said. "Come over here." As Bill kept on going down the rubber mat toward the dressing room he saw Wares was talking very seriously. He couldn't hear what it was but Moore's face suddenly reddened.

The morning had one more surprise. Coming on top of everything else, it simply left Bill a little numb.

After a practice nobody was inclined to hurry much. They'd hurried to get up, eat, walk to the rink, practise. Now the morning stretched ahead. But there did seem to be abnormal activity around the dressing room. The trainer had a big trunk packed and locked near the door and was packing another. "Some of you guys are going to have clammy equipment tonight," he muttered once, almost to himself, "But we can't help that."

And then he went around to a few amateurs and told them the coach wanted to see them. Bill looked at the ones who were called. Carson, a defenceman from Alberta. Givens – he looked saddest of all. Waddington, a willowy centre from Ottawa. Connelly and Ortona from somewhere in the Maritimes. They knew what it was and took it with wry grimaces, but not much surprise. Carson took it hardest. He'd come a long way. On the way out to see the coach, he stopped by the door. He had freckles and red hair and rather a bony face. "If I don't see some of you guys again for a while," he called, "good luck anyway. Nice knowing you." There were friendly calls in reply.

The five had gone, Bill knew, to be told that they weren't needed any longer. When it came to him, maybe next week – *if* it came, he thought fiercely – he wondered how he'd take it. And how would the coach say it?

When they were gone, the trainer took a couple of sheets of typed paper out of a big brown envelope. Without saying anything, he went and taped them to the inside of the door. Bill wanted to jump and be first to read them. But the Leafs were holding back, treating it casually, until finally Otto Tihane went over and had a look. Then a trickle. Then a flood of the younger ones. And there it was: Bill Spunska was on the roster of the Toronto Maple Leafs.

When he walked back to his seat, he tried to keep calm. They had to put me somewhere, he thought. It had to be either St. Catharines or the Leafs. Doesn't mean a thing, at this stage. They had fourteen defencemen to split up and couldn't put all the good ones on one team.

But he couldn't help it. He could see the story in the Winnipeg papers, could hear the kids at the Northwest talking about it Monday, Sarah and Pete and Mother and Dad looking in disbelief. As well they should, he warned himself soberly.

He couldn't help himself, though. He grinned from ear to ear. When Otto Tihane spoke to him, he just grinned. When Jim Butt came along and said, "Hey! Spunska of the Leafs, eh?" Bill shook his head and tried to say something, but all he could do was grin, ear to ear.

CHAPTER 11 ▬

At noon, Pamela Moore was relieved on the desk. Usually, the time shot by when she was working, but this morning had been difficult. Every time someone entered the lobby she'd looked up sharply to see if he looked like a local newspaperman. That business last night. . . . She felt sick every time she thought of it. But there had been nothing about it in the morning paper from Toronto. No mention of it around the lobby that she had heard. Still, the police *had* been involved. They'd asked her all those questions. She hadn't even seen Benny this morning. The look on his face last night when the man at the pool said he was phoning the police – she hoped she never would see that look on anyone's face again: shock, despair, and then the defiance most familiar to everybody connected with him, people who didn't know that he ever felt anything but defiance.

She needed a Coke. Or some coffee. She hadn't been able to eat this morning. If only she could talk to someone about it! If only someone was on her side, on Benny's side! Someone who would just listen. . . .

The clerk who had relieved her was busy at the desk. Once he turned to her. "What's the matter, don't you want to go?" he asked, and smiled. She tried to smile back. She was standing by the switchboard. There weren't any players in the lobby. Benny hadn't come back from the morning practice, either. That worried her.

What she did next was entirely on impulse. She plugged a line into Room 309. A voice answered. She asked, "Bill?"

"Speaking," he said.

She could see him the way he'd be – big, dark, and serious, and yet sometimes with a flash of wit or understanding. She was a lively girl and boys often kidded her. He never had. Yet she had a feeling that he was glad to see her every time they met. She knew that lighting up in a man's face.

"It's Pam," she said. She tried to think of something to ask him, some kidding that would be an excuse for phoning. She couldn't. In a subdued voice she said, "This is silly, but I . . . but I . . ."

Bill, sitting on his bed, listening to her fumble for words, knew that something was wrong. He forgot his own elation all of a sudden, thought about that hastily stopping taxi last night, the sprint Benny Moore had made to get in, the fact that earlier Pam had been going to meet him but hadn't returned with him. . . . "Want me to come down?" he asked. "I'll buy you a Coke, okay?"

"Okay," she said.

He buttoned his collar quickly, tied his tie, picked up his jacket. He didn't wait for the elevator but went down the stairs. She was standing a few feet in front of the desk. She was wearing a dark linen suit this morning and looked very pretty. "Hi," he said.

"Is it warm enough to walk without a coat?" she asked.

"Sure," he said, a little surprised that she wanted to go out. "Let's go."

They turned left, coming out of the hotel. Players were going in and out. They turned and looked and kidded Bill. Nothing was private on a hockey team. Tim Merrill winked at him and said, "You might not be very old, William, but you're very lucky!" Bill smiled back. So did Pam. But he noticed that her smile was a little different today. Usually it lingered a while. This morning when she stopped smiling it was like turning out a light and no brightness was left.

A block away, they turned to the right along the main street, staying in the warmth of the sunny side. They crossed with a light. The crowds hurried by or loafed by looking in windows.

She said, "I had to talk to someone."

"What's the matter?" he asked, looking down at her. He didn't ask *if* something was the matter. He thought: If nothing was the matter, we wouldn't be here.

"Do you happen to know if Benny got in on time last night?" she asked, hesitantly. "I mean, was anything said about it this morning, that you heard?"

What was this about? He couldn't guess. "I happened to be looking out of the window when he came in," he said. "He made it."

"Did you hear anything else?" She was looking at him anxiously. "Anything about him this morning, I mean?"

He was a little slow to answer. He wasn't a gossip by nature. He'd seen the way the pros did it, the men he admired, was to leave the small private things behind in the dressing room. But this was a little different. So he told Pam about the coach calling Benny aside when they were coming off the ice. "I don't know what he said," Bill said. "Then in the dressing room he was a lot later than the rest of us, because I guess he was talking to the coach for a while. There were a couple of fellows waiting . . ."

"Dark? About the same size?" she exclaimed.

He nodded.

"Those two!" she said.

"What's it all about?" he asked.

"He lived with them last year when he was here. At least, he was supposed to be in the boarding house with the other players, but these two had this apartment and they used to have the players up there for parties some times. I know Benny used to sleep there half the time, too." They walked on for half a block before she spoke again. "Did you know that you and Benny are going to be moved in together tomorrow?"

Bill stopped in the middle of the sidewalk and two old ladies almost knocked him down from behind.

"It's true!" Pam said. "Mr. Wares brought down the new lists this morning, because he won't be back until late tonight. It doesn't take effect until tomorrow, to give the ones who've been cut a chance to move out." She looked at him suddenly, rather shyly. "By the way – congratulations!" She meant for surviving the cut, and Bill thanked her. . . . But Benny Moore, his roommate!

But after the first shock, he thought – this was strange – he'd almost expected something like this. It was just like the coach to take two men who were trying to knock each other into the rail seats every time they met and make them roommates. He grinned. Wouldn't the sportswriters and the scouts have a great time with that?

"You didn't hear anything more?" Pam probed. "Anything those two said to Benny, or anything?"

Bill shook his head, thoughtfully.

"I wish I knew whether it'll be in the local paper!" she said despairingly.

Bill couldn't stand it any longer. "Look!" he said. "I just don't know what you're talking about!"

She looked at him for a long few seconds. "I'll tell you," she said. "It'll get out. He needs *some-body*. . . . You're not mad at him, are you?" she asked in some alarm.

"No," Bill said, slowly. But it was a poser. They had forgotten about the Coke. That had been just an excuse, anyway. Was he mad at Benny Moore? Across the street was a little park and beyond that a school. The park was full of students – older students, some older than Bill and Pam – having lunch. There was a spare bench. They sat on it.

"I'm not mad at him," Bill said. "But he seems mad at me, although I don't know why he should stay mad so long!"

"That's him!" she sighed. "You know when you saw me going out last night? I'd had a call

from him. They'd decided to go swimming."
She hesitated. "One of the others, Tom Amadio
his name is, has asked me out several times. I
don't go, because all their parties wind up back
at that apartment and they're older than I am
and. . . . Well, I just don't go. But this time
Benny phoned. He said they had two girls and
needed one more – and, well, I wasn't doing
anything, so I went."

Bill was still, listening. She had very clear
skin. Her hands were surprisingly strong looking
and firm. So were her legs – shapely but sturdy,
not willowy.

"So we went swimming," she said. "There's
this pool, heated, and it was all sort of fun." She
paused. "I mean, I know you couldn't know my
brother the way I do. But, well, he's *my*
brother. He's looked after me when I needed it.
And last night there was another group there
and they recognized him and they said something. This happens all the time, to him. They
said nothing very bad, but just the kind of thing
people say to Benny – 'Think you can lead that
league in penalties too?' That sort of thing. It's
sort of his form of recognition, do you see?"

"Yes," Bill said slowly. And now that Pam
said it, he did see. He hadn't at all, before.

"So one of them called him over to where they
were. You know, it's sort of slippery around a
pool. The rest of us – the two other girls, I

didn't know them well . . ." she let that go, ". . . and Tom and the other man, Johnny, his name is – were just sitting there watching. This boy put his hand on Benny's arm and was looking over my way and said something, and suddenly Benny jerked his arm around. He was just wrenching it free, really, but the other fellow hung on and just seemed to leap through the air, and then slid, and fell, and hit his shoulder and head against the side of the diving tower!"

"Did Benny tell you what the fellow said?" Bill asked.

She nodded her head. Bill waited. "It wasn't so bad," she said finally, faltering a little. "I mean, it wasn't so bad even compared to what I've heard Benny and Tom and Johnny say, when they're talking about some other girl. But this was about me. I guess that's what made the difference. He just said if Benny ever wanted to get rid of that red-haired broad, to let him know." She looked at Bill, wry amusement in her eyes.

"So the manager came running out. He said he'd seen the whole thing. That Benny had flung the other fellow against the diving tower and that he was going to call the police!"

"What did Benny say then?"

She said slowly, "He took a step toward the manager. I thought he was going to hit him.

You know how red his face gets. He even had his fist clenched. But then he stopped. But the man had seen the move he'd made and he just turned and ran. A little later the police got there. And do you know what the other man said, the one who'd made the remark about me? He said Benny had made a nasty remark about one of the girls he was with, and he'd told Benny to take off and Benny had knocked him into the diving tower! And the pool manager, all he did was stand there saying, 'These pro hockey players, they're all alike. Think they can shove anybody around, think they're big shots, or something! And Benny Moore is the worst of the lot!' Things like that." Her eyes suddenly were brimming. "I'm just afraid that if the police believe that man, there'll be trouble, and if Benny gets into more trouble he won't have any chance in hockey – you know that. Nobody really wants to take a chance on him, now, except Mr. Wares!"

Bill sat there. He could see the scene she had described. It could happen – it must have happened that way, or she wouldn't have told him.

"I told the police that," she said. "Benny pleaded with them, too. I've never seen him plead with anyone before. But he pleaded with them please to let him get into a taxi and get back before the curfew. 'If I break it, I'm sunk!'

he kept saying. He really cares, Bill. I know he must act like a crazy man sometimes. I know it! But he really cares!"

"What can I do?" Bill asked.

"You're going to room with him. This thing will get into the papers somehow. If there's been pressure on him before, it's going to be even worse now." They were sitting a foot or so apart on the bench. She reached over and put her hand on his arm and left it there.

Bill got the message: Great! I'm supposed to become a friend to a guy who keeps knocking my head off every time I look down when we're on the ice.

Yet he remembered the times when he had caught on Benny Moore's face expressions that were not the usual: the twinge of envy that he, Spunska, was rooming with Tim Merrill; the uncertainty on that morning when he came into the breakfast room; the inquiry about the bump on Bill's head – that he, Moore, had caused.

"I'll do what I can," Bill said. "It might not be much – but I'll do what I can."

She said simply, "Thanks."

They sat a few minutes longer. Then they got up and walked back. For more than half an hour, Bill had forgotten the principal fact of to-day. He remembered only when they were back at the hotel. Jim Butt was in the lobby looking for him. "Hey!" he said. "Didn't you know we're supposed to have steaks in a few minutes and get the bus for this game? We're playing, you know! You and me! Butt and Spunska, the newest Leafs!"

"Sounds like a vaudeville team to me," a voice said. "Butt and Spunska, indeed!" Squib Jackson poked them both on the way by. "Products of good scouting," he said calmly. "No credit due either of you, at all."

Pam looked at Bill. "Thanks," she said. "I'll be going . . ."

When she started away, Butt looked at Bill and when he saw the look on Bill's face decided it wasn't a joking matter, and let it slide. Bill called after Pam, and went to her.

"Why don't you tell the coach?" he asked.

"What?" she faltered.

"Exactly what you told me," he said. "Including the fact that Benny always has protected you."

CHAPTER 12 ◀

Bill later was to remember that day for a lot more than this talk with Pam, his first road trip, his first game with the Leafs. For years later, he'd remember it as the day most of the Leafs first set eyes on Zingo Zubek. It was the first day all except Bill had even heard of Zingo Zubek in fact. Although Zingo himself later always denied that it was possible for a man to grow up in this country without having heard of Zingo Zubek – even, as he said, "You ingrown toenails from the East." Bill had, of course. Zingo had played for Kelvin in the Winnipeg high school league.

Everything was by schedule. The itinerary posted by the elevator told it all.

2 p.m.   Steaks for players on Leafs' roster.
2:30 p.m.   Bus picks up equipment trunks at
            Arena.
3 p.m.   Bus leaves front of Empress Hotel for
            St. Catharines. All players on Leafs'
            roster on board.

The players on the St. Catharines roster were working out again this afternoon, so the group in the dining room was only half the normal size. As they finished eating, most of the players took some fruit from a big bowl – a couple of apples, bananas, pears, peaches, grapes.

Bill had never seen fruit in such profusion. Of course, it was sold in Manitoba, but . . . well, it cost money. It was almost a luxury in some homes. Including his. He couldn't decide.

"Why don't you take the bowl?" Otto Tihanc asked him. Bill wouldn't do that. But Merv McGarry would. He picked it up as was and was starting out the door with it when one of the hostesses shrieked, "Mr. McGarry!"

McGarry put the fruit bowl on another table and pretended to bolt. Then he came back and selected a peach and an apple. Bill took the same. Out of the hotel. Straight into the big air-conditioned bus with green-tinted windows. Because of the byplay over the fruit bowl Bill found that he was almost the last one onto the bus. He took a seat near the front with Jim Butt. The players seemed to have accepted now that Spunska and Butt, the rookies, hung together.

Bill gave Butt part of a Toronto newspaper. "Read that story on the sports pages about Zingo Zubek," he said. "Ever hear of him?"

"No," Butt said.

Bill laughed. "I've played against him. Read it."

Jim ran his eyes over the headlines and

stopped at one that said: PINT-SIZED PLAYER
GETS CHANCE TONIGHT.

It was a story from St. Catharines about the
game between Chicago and Toronto there
tonight, and read:

ST. CATHARINES, Sept. 18 – "It might not be the
humane thing to do," said Black Mike Foster,
coach of the Black Hawks, "but I'm not sure who
should be the ones to worry – us or the Leafs. So I'm
going to give Zingo Zubek a chance to play
tonight."

Zingo was christened Lorne, but says he's been
known as Zingo to everyone since his first appear-
ance on skates in a public school game in Edmonton a few years ago. He is the fastest man in the
Chicago camp and poses a real problem for coach
Foster – who says he brought Zubek to camp almost
as a gag. "My scouts insisted," he said. But Zingo
scored four goals in one workout earlier this week
and has yet to have a scrimmage where he hasn't
scored. He played high school hockey last year in
Winnipeg but moved up to junior when the high
school league season ended. He also played one season of junior hockey in Edmonton before moving to
Winnipeg a year ago.

Zingo really is an oddity in a game which isn't
impossible for small players – but as his coach says,
"Not that small!" Zingo weighs only 130 pounds.
He's five feet five and nineteen years old. He insists
his size doesn't handicap him any. "I'm too small
for those big guys to hit," he says. "They take aim,

throw a check, and when they're still looking up their sleeves to see where I went I'm in shooting at their goal."

Nobody ever accused Zingo of being modest. He's never met a defence yet that he couldn't tie in reef knots; even in the Chicago camp, some days. People here are wondering if the cocky little guy finally will meet his match in such as Otto Tihane, Tim Merrill, and others on the Leafs' defence. In fact, they've been wondering about it so much that the Arena is likely to be a sellout for tonight.

In the crowd also will be two men who are visiting the hockey camps right now looking for players who are willing to go to the University of British Columbia and play hockey on what will become Canada's Olympic hockey team. They are Josh Paddock and Professor Hector Mahoney of UBC. They have expressed a great deal of interest in Zubek. They also will be watching Jim Butt on the Leafs tonight, because Butt, a good prospect but unlikely to make the Leafs, is known to be interested in a university education.

When Jim finished reading, Bill looked at him. "Have these fellows from UBC talked to you?" he asked.

Butt shook his head. "All I know is what I read in the papers." He grinned. "Might not be a bad thing, though. Good school. And the climate is about the best in the country. Next to Victoria. But that's in B.C. too, of course, a little farther south and on the island."

"Would they give you board and room and everything?"

"I don't know."

They all noticed Zingo Zubek in the warm-up. He was a bandy-legged little guy and took short thrusts with his skates, a queer way of skating, bent over so that he seemed even shorter than he was. He skated jerkily, like a toy or an automatic man. His hair was dark and cut short and plastered like a skull cap to his head. He had a wide mouth and thin lips with a kind of humorous twist to them.

One foghorn-voiced fan in the Arena yelled, "What's this team the Leafs are playing, anyway – the Singer midgets?"

Zubek dropped his stick, clapped both his hands over his head like a fighter, and bowed.

But for the first period neither Chicago nor the Leafs used any new players. These teams had met in the Stanley Cup playoffs the year before. While this was just an exhibition, it was apparent that neither of the coaches particularly wanted to lose any games, even exhibitions. Anson Oakley flitted through the Chicago defence for a backhand goal in the first minute of the first period. Pete Pollock got it back for Chicago with a shot from the blueline that went in off a skate.

Down at the end of the Toronto bench sat Bill Spunska and Jim Butt, watching the play go up and down. When the buzzer ended the period, Jim rose and stretched. "I feel like going for a skate between periods to limber up," he said. They clumped down the passageway to the dressing room at the end of the line. Since neither had played junior in these parts, there were many curious gazes in their direction. One woman who looked near sixty, except that her hair was flaming red, leaned over the alleyway and said politely to Bill in the buzz of voices, "What would your name be, young fellow?"

"Bill Spunska," he said, as politely.

"Eh?" she called.

He repeated his name. She still didn't get it. "Write it here," she said. He did. Then Butt yelled at him to hurry – and he just made it in before the dressing room door closed. He didn't know what he had expected between periods in an NHL game to be like. But maybe because this was an exhibition, it seemed quite a bit like the ones back in high school. Some players were taking off their skates. Everybody was leaning back against the wall.

"Hardly got warmed up," complained Otto Tihane, next to him.

Bill grinned. "*You* hardly got warmed up!"

Johnny Bosfield, the goalie, grinned. "You got twenty years, kid. Take it easy!"

Pokesy Wares didn't come into the room until near the end of the intermission.

Jim Butt and Bill were standing up, talking. "Is that a hint, or something?" Pokesy demanded. "Showing me you're tired sitting?"

In the second period Bill was back on the end of the bench. But just being here, in a Leaf sweater with that big number on the back, was almost enough. In fact, he was sort of glad he hadn't been put out there in the first period. He'd heard sometimes that when a player had been injured and was almost ready to play, it wasn't a bad idea for him to sit on the bench for a couple of games just to get him back into the feeling of being on the team. Bill felt something of this now. The low-voiced chatter along the bench came to him. "I thought the ref was going to nail me on that one, my stick got caught in his sweater. . . ." "Notice the stick Jackman is using? He's taken more off the blade than last year." And occasional cries to the men on the ice – "Go, go!" "Look out, meathead!" "Shoot, shoot!"

About half through the period, Leafs got two fast goals. Maniscola and Merrill. Now they led 3–1. And off the Chicago bench came Zubek, playing left wing.

"Butt!" called Pokesy. "Take right wing. Oakley centre. Maniscola left." He thus put a rookie against a rookie. Butt against Zubek. When Spunska saw Butt go out with that long powerful stride he thought, Zubek will have to be pretty good to get away from him.

"Spunska, right defence!"

When his name was called he was thinking of Butt and Zubek. Before Wares had finished saying the word "defence," Bill was over the boards, landing clumsily in an eager, headlong leap, skating toward the blueline, adjusting his gloves. Old Buff Koska, coming off, tapped the seat of Bill's pants with his stick. Tihane was on left defence.

The face-off after the second of the two quick goals was at centre ice. Zingo Zubek loafed back into his own zone waiting for the play. Then, convoyed closely by Butt, he came back through the centre zone, bandy-legged, jerky. He seemed to be going nowhere. His centre was coming up fast with the puck. Bill and Tihane, on the blueline, made ready. The pass came over to Zubek. It looked too far ahead. But the little legs pumped suddenly. He pulled away from Jim, took the pass, headed for the boards. Bill went with him, skating hard, arms wide, intending to skate Zubek into the boards, smother the play there. He had committed himself when Zubek cut in. Bill lunged back, missed with a poke check. Zubek cut out again but this time Butt was on him, so Zubek passed to the right wing, in the corner. Then he dashed for the goal, Bill with him, never letting him get set. The puck came out. Zubek stopped it. Bill lunged wildly and knocked it away.

Jiggs Maniscola picked it up, wheeled in front of the defence and headed with Butt and Oakley for the other blueline. Zubek loafed along behind Butt, taking those short strides. Jiggs passed to Oakley who was flying in over the Chicago blueline. He shot. The goalie, up from the farm system, a tall thin boy with fair hair, kicked it out. Butt was cutting in fast. The puck was there, but rolling. Just as Jim was about to golf it back at the goal, Zubek suddenly went around him and came out the other side with the puck, passed to his centre man, was knocked down by the startled Butt, was up like a rubber ball, and the play was wheeling in on the Toronto defence again.

In a few seconds the lines began to change, and Bill was watching Zubek from the bench. He'd been tough enough when he was with Kelvin. Here he seemed twice as hard to catch.

Wares was behind him. "Don't commit yourself so fast," he said. "Just slow him up, let the wing get back." He paused a minute. "You'll get another chance against him."

Next time Zingo came to the ice he skated past the Toronto bench and called, "Okay, Pokesy – you can send out the rookies again."

Bill could hear Butt growl something under

his breath, as he took up his patrol, checking Zubek.

Butt seemed a foot taller than Zubek. Of course he wasn't, but with Zubek's hunched style it looked that way. He planted himself a stride ahead of Zubek right from where the puck was dropped. He stayed there. He intercepted passes. He slapped them away. He wouldn't leave Zubek alone for an instant. For that line change it worked. Bill breathed easier. Next time they were on it worked, too. Zubek had done nothing since the first near miss. He seemed to be just going through the motions, skating up and down his wing with Jim Butt so close they sometimes seemed like one four-elbowed hockey player. Right at the end of the period Jim Butt picked up a pass and decided to do some rolling on his own. He turned. There was that sudden burst of speed again, a blur – and Zubek had the puck, clear of Jim, and was coming in on Bill again, yelling, "Look out, kid!" Bill didn't swing so wide this time. He tried to stay close enough to the boards to swing out if Zubek went that way, or to swing in if Zubek swung in. He watched the little guy's eyes as he came in, clicked a pass to centre, squirted along the boards past Bill, cut in fast. Bill got his stick on the return pass, started to carry it out. Zubek swirled like a swallow, stole the puck, was in the clear again, set himself for a shot, and passed at the last instant to Norman barging in hard from the other wing. Bosfield just got over in time to make the save.

Between periods that time there was a certain amount of talk about Zubek. "Good shift!" "So darn small I can hardly see him, let alone hit him." "One good body check and he wouldn't get up until spring." "Okay, let's see you hit him." And from Annie Oakley, a tricky skater himself, a tribute: "I wish I could move it like he does."

It was 3–1 going into the third, but Chicago scored off the opening face-off and it was still 3–2 with three minutes to go. The second lines of both teams fought it out for a minute. Then the third lines for another minute. With seventy seconds left there was a line change again. Bill was on the defence. The face-off was in the Chicago zone. The pass went back to Maniscola. Bill and Otto moved up to the blueline to hold it in. Bill got a shot. Otto got one. Then a pass went wrong and a defenceman slapped it up to Zubek.

Bill saw him coming and he knew that if he missed this body check Zubek would be in the clear. So he didn't body-check. He turned and dug in to get back. He could hear Zubek coming behind him. And he heard from the crowd not cheers – but laughter! He glanced around.

Zubek was six feet behind him. Bill swung his stick back on the right side and Zubek danced out of the way. Bill swung it on the left. The laughter rose. They were over the blueline. Now Bill had to turn, in front of his net, to spoil this shot. He saw the others coming back fast as he took one last look over his shoulder. Then he faked a turn to his right, but turned to his left instead and met Zubek head on. It could have been a tougher check, but he knocked Zubek down and that was enough. The puck was there. He slapped it to Jiggs and the play went down to the Chicago net.

Zubek bounced up. He slammed his stick on the ice in disgust. That time it had been just the two of them, Bill Spunska and Zingo Zubek. And Bill had got him.

"You're not bad, kid," he said to Bill. "But I wouldn't fall for that fake turn again."

Bill just grinned. "I'd hate to have to beat you all the time," he said.

"What was the laughing about?" he asked Jim in the dressing room after the game.

"The little guy was clowning when he was following you down! Every time you looked over your right shoulder he swung to the left. When you looked that way he swung to the right. And all the time grinning."

"He's some hockey player!" Bill said.

Wares came along just then and overheard. "You hit him, didn't you? If he's some hockey player, you must be a little better, eh?"

Bill looked at him, smiling a little. He felt the colour move up in his face.

"I saw that shift you gave him, as if you're going to turn one way. Where'd you learn that?"

Bill looked at Otto Tihane, who was grinning, rather pleased.

"Ott showed me the other day," Bill said. "Like for when I'm going into a corner after a puck and a guy is behind me, to try to make him think I'm going the other way."

The trainer had stopped by the coach. "Pokes," he said. "Those two from UBC are out there waiting. . . ."

"Let 'em come in," Merv McGarry called. "We could use a little tone around this club."

"To heck with that!" Pokesy said. "Nuts to letting 'em come in! Anybody who's trying out for Toronto Maple Leafs is trying out for Toronto Maple Leafs, not for any university professors. Anybody I cut, they're welcome to talk to! Anybody who's trying to make it with my club either doesn't think of any other club, or they can get off right now. Any questions?"

There were no questions. At first Bill thought maybe it was a little drastic. Take Butt, for instance. He wasn't even a longshot bet to make the Leafs this year. If he'd rather play college hockey than go to the minors, why couldn't he talk to the men from UBC? But, as the coach had said, Leafs had paid their way down here and were supporting them. And with the Olympics nearly eighteen months away, it wasn't as if there wasn't time.

Funny thing! He'd been sitting here undressing just as if this happened every day. Suddenly he realized: Hey, I just played my first game for the Leafs!

He grinned. Tihane caught the eyes of a couple of other players and jerked his head toward Bill. When Bill looked up, eight or ten players all were looking at him and grinning.

"You did okay, kid," Buff Koska said, from across the room.

It was like getting a medal.

CHAPTER 13 ▬

"Bored?"

Bill looked up. He'd been so sleepy when he staggered stiffly in from the bus at three a.m. that he'd forgotten to pick up his mail. Now it was nearly noon and he was in the lobby reading it when Jiggs Maniscola asked the question. No workouts today. A light skate, and even that was over now.

Bill smiled. "Not really," he said. "To tell the truth, I guess . . ." he stopped and then finished with a rush, "I guess I'm just having too good a time to get bored."

Maniscola dropped into a chair beside him. "What are the clippings?"

Bill passed them over. They had come with a letter from his dad and mother and were from the Winnipeg papers.

One headline read: SPUNSKA TAKES ON BAD BENNY MOORE. The letter from his father, in referring to the clippings, asked, "What's this all about, son?"

Sometimes Bill wished he knew.

After he had handed the one story, a wire service report, to Maniscola, Bill kept on reading another clipping. It was from Lee Vincent's column in the Winnipeg *Telegram*. Lee started out by referring to the wire service story that had been carried elsewhere in the sports pages that day. He'd phoned a scout he knew in the Leafs' camp to get more details.

His column read:

Apparently, it's not all bad. Pokesy Wares, the Leafs' coach, was quoted by a radio station one night this way: "They're both good young defencemen. They like to hit, and a lot of this game is hitting. I'll tell you one thing, this is a better hockey camp at this stage because of these two. It's keeping everybody else awake." He said that some day those two might wind up playing defence together somewhere in the Toronto system – and that if he was a forward then he'd think about three times before he tried to go through between them.

But the pro hockey writers have kept the thing going, with enthusiasm. Usually the first weeks of training are dull for them. Now they've all done features on Moore, the bad boy who wants so much to make good. And on Spunska, the kid from our Winnipeg high school league who was the first player any of them could remember coming straight from high school and making this good a run at a job with the Leafs. Not that he'll make it this year, they said – but that colour! Those body checks! When he gets a little more experience, they think, he'll be a good one.

We could have told them that, eh?

Maniscola read the clipping and then got up. Squib Jackson was coming across the lobby, looking out of the window at the quiet Sunday streets. "Hey, your young guy here is getting famous," Jiggs said to the scout, passing him the clipping.

Squib read it, twitching his mustache now and again. Then he passed it back, without comment.

It was funny. They were only starting Bill's second week in camp. But already the tension was beginning to build about what would happen at the end of this week. Bill looked up suddenly, his thoughts interrupted by some movement near the desk. But it wasn't Pam. He hadn't seen her today. He went back to thinking about breakfast. He and Givens and Butt once again had been talking about where they went from here. Givens was leaving today to wait for the junior season to start. "I'm ready," Butt said, laughing, when they were talking about the fact that some of the older players were talking contract with the coach. "If the coach only knew it, a contract discussion as far as I'm concerned is, he hauls out a piece of paper and I sign it."

He and Bill were among the ones who really expected to be cut sooner or later – the main question being, cut to where? They still had junior hockey left before the age limit of twenty would cut them off. Mr. Jackson had been with them, at breakfast. Bill and Jim had said frankly that they'd been wondering where did they go from here if *they* were cut?

"That's where the ticklish part comes," the scout said, hunting for a cigarette. "There's some of you kids – well, I'm not talking about you – but some kids that look just about good enough to turn pro, but I don't think we should make a decision like that at this stage of the camp. You turn a kid pro before he's ready, and he sits on the bench for a year with Leafs or down in the minors and it doesn't do him any good. He's far better off back home playing junior and getting lots of ice time. Or you can send him down to a league where he technically isn't a pro but like in the juniors he gets paid all right and makes enough to live on and gets lots of experience." He seemed to be thinking out loud. "And then at this stage of the camp, too, there's always injuries. You send a kid home now, and in three or four days you might not have enough players for some of the exhibition games we've got coming up."

"How many are going to be cut next weekend?" Bill asked.

Suddenly Squib seemed to have decided that he had been talking too much. "Well, it's not up to me," he said. "But probably there'd be eight or ten sent out. Meanwhile, you get a kick out of being on the Leafs' roster?"

"I certainly do!" Bill said.

He'd learned quite a bit in one week, playing with professionals. There had been a lot of difference in skill between him and the good youngsters in the high school league in Winnipeg when he first started out. That was nothing to the gap that spread between him and these players. Every minute on the ice reinforced his sobering knowledge that he had a vast distance to go before he could be considered in the same class at all.

Squib said, "Well, you wouldn't be on that roster if you hadn't made an impression on the coach. But, I don't think you're going to stay on that roster very long – maybe not more than a week. We wanted to split up the young guys that were left, after we sent the rest of them home. That meant you either had to go on Leafs' or St. Catharines. There ain't no others."

Squib was about to say that St. Catharines had put up a big argument to get Moore, then decided not to. He might tell Moore, just in case information of this kind might help the kid find a sense of responsibility. But no use telling Spunska. "I think you can take it as read that some of those fellows on the St. Catharines roster are going to wind up with the Leafs either this year or next, and some of the ones on the Leafs' roster are going to wind up down there. But I will say one thing. The coach knows pretty well what most of the pros will do. By putting you others into a few exhibition games he can get a better idea of how you react against pro opposition." He was tempted to go on and tell Bill that it was a pretty good bet that he was going to be made to look like a very green young man in some of those exhibition games and that he shouldn't let it bother him. But again he decided that was better unsaid. Let the kid find out the hard things himself.

Bill said, "I don't care really how I happened to get on that roster but . . ." He couldn't say any more. Sufficient unto the day is the joy therein and all that sort of thing.

A little later, Squib strolled off across the lobby. Then Tommy Nathanson and Bobby Deyell and Dan Carsen, the three trainers, came over. They had been at the rink unpacking and drying the equipment from last night's game. Bill enjoyed the casual atmosphere of this day. Everything had moved so rapidly all week that they hadn't had much time to fill in the odd gaps, find out little things. Deyell was talking about the letters sent to players who were coming to camp.

Bill remembered. "I meant to ask," he said, "what was meant by that part about bringing any special protective equipment I had. I had some stuff but Mr. Jackson told me that would all be supplied and I didn't quite know . . ."

Deyell laughed. "No, that's because kids maybe have trick knees, or elbows, or something like that. If they've had special braces made, there's no use them coming down here and wearing other ones that don't fit. Sometimes if a kid wastes a few days of training getting a brace fitted or something like that he never does catch up. You don't look as if there's anything much the matter with you anyway."

Tommy Nathanson, the skates specialist, chuckled. "He's only about fourteen," he said. "There shouldn't be anything the matter with him."

Bill smiled. "Eighteen and a half."

Old Tommy said, "You're growing up. A lot of guys would say, 'Nearly nineteen.' Maybe you're a little smarter than you look. The first thing some old hockey players wish they'd done is falsify their age by about three years downward. Most of them don't realize that until they're in their twenties. There are two or three guys around this league who I think are about forty-five, and the record books show they're thirty-seven."

"Quit talking about Johnny Bosfield," Merv McGarry said, joining the group.

Deyell jabbed McGarry a hard one in the ribs.

"I'll see you at the golf club this afternoon," Deyell said, rising. "Remember, one o'clock."

"Don't chicken out," McGarry said. "I want your money."

McGarry said, "You know, when I came into the league, there weren't any nice guys around like me to look after rookies and crack jokes for them and make them feel at home. I really had to fight my way along."

Pokesy Wares was passing. "If you'd had to fight your way along, McGarry," the coach said, "you never would have got here."

McGarry yelled after him, "You taking a recess in all that handing out raises you're doing?"

They were sitting there – McGarry, Nathanson, Carsen, and Bill – when Benny Moore came into the lobby. When Bill saw Moore, immediately he had the same kind of feeling as when he was waiting for a puck carrier to come to him at the blueline – a sort of getting ready, getting set. Moore was dressed in a sober blue blazer with the crest of some hockey club on the pocket. His grey flannels were nicely cut, exactly the kind of pants that Bill would like to own. A pair of shiny black loafers and black socks, white shirt, and knitted blue tie made up the rest of it. To look at him you'd think, Bill thought, he was a member of a country club.

The two dark men were with him. They were both quite a bit older, and there was a sharpy look to them that induced in Bill a bit of uneasiness. He couldn't identify that either because he wasn't well enough informed in what adults were like, or rather in forming judgements of adults, to be sure exactly what he felt. But there was a type of man his father and mother always regarded rather watchfully. These two were of that type. The three of them were laughing and chatting as they arrived at the elevator, where the two team rosters now were posted.

Bill noticed that Moore scarcely glanced at the rosters. He'd known what was on them since yesterday. But apparently the other men didn't. One – would he be the one who was always asking Pam out? – took a look. He was smoking a cigar. He took it out of his mouth and flung it into a tall sand-filled ashtray that stood by the elevator. He threw the cigar so hard that sand spattered out onto the floor. From across the lobby people watching could hear his ejaculation: "That punk kid, with the Leafs!"

Bill stiffened. McGarry put one hand over and laid it on Bill's arm. "Keep cool," he said.

The trainers sat silently, watchful. The man turned and saw Bill. He said something more.

The elevator came. The three of them walked in. The doors slid closed and the moment was past.

McGarry broke the silence. "That should be an interesting exhibition game here on Tuesday night," he said innocently. "St. Catharines versus the Leafs, or, Moore versus Spunska – the battle of the century."

Bill grinned a little but said nothing.

The others gradually drifted away. Bill sat loosely in the big chair, his elbows resting on the arms and his hands resting lightly on his knees. He was thinking: In all the day-dreaming I did about this camp back in the summer there were some things I didn't foresee. Benny Moore was one of them.

And yet when he sat there, he had that feeling of somebody coming in on defence and the play was either knock down or be knocked down. That was the game.

CHAPTER 14 ▄

After all that, becoming Benny Moore's roommate wasn't anything like as difficult a matter as it had looked at first. Benny simply moved in, later in the day. He arrived at the door with his bags, grinned, and said, "This must be the same kind of idea that somebody had when they put Daniel in the lion's den, eh?" And later when he was putting his stuff away, he said, "My kid sister tells me that I'm to be nice to you, or she'll clobber me herself."

Bill said, "Those pals of yours didn't seem awfully pleased that I'm even alive."

Benny was standing at the window. He turned and he wasn't smiling. "Oh, them . . ." he said, and stopped. He shrugged and let it drop.

There was silence for half an hour. Bill was writing a letter to Sarah. He missed her and the easy friendship they'd had for nearly two years now, the way they talked to one another about things they didn't tell others. "Funny how two people from the same family can be so different," he wrote at the end of a paragraph about Benny Moore. "His sister, Pam, the redhead I told you about in my last letter, is really nice."

He stared at the sentence and wondered. Would Sarah think he and Pam had something going? He didn't think so. Anyway, they hadn't. A little postscript appeared in his mind: not yet, anyway. Then he thought of how he had felt last year, the time she went out with Cliff Armstrong. Yet he and Sarah had talked about things like this. Her letters from Banff in the summer, when she'd been working there as a waitress and he'd been in Toronto, had mentioned this guy or that, some favourably. Sometimes when they were together they felt very tender towards one another, but sometimes they were more like just really close friends. He shrugged and sealed the envelope.

Moore was lying fully dressed on the bed that had been Tim Merrill's. He was in exactly the same position as he'd been almost exactly one week before, that first night, when Bill walked in and found him stretched out on that bed, smoking a cigar.

"You're a little crazy yourself," Moore mused. "Had you noticed that?"

Bill shook his head, wondering what was coming.

"It takes a bit of a crazy guy to play the game the way you do," Moore said. "I've watched you in the workouts. You have one big idea at a time. You are going to stop a guy, say. So okay, if you have to stop him five times before you get him, you're going to stop him. If you are rushing you don't stop until you ram the end of the rink. I hear that the first time that Zubek came in on you you made about four separate passes at him before he surrendered."

"He never surrendered," Bill said. "That guy . . ."

"I know," Moore said. "I played against him two years ago in Edmonton in an exhibition. Nobody ever made me look more stupid than Zubek did." He said this with remarkable calm. "One time he was coming in and I decided that I would finish him for that game, if it cost me a five-minute penalty. I cross-checked him. Or I tried to. Did you ever try to cross-check a bunny rabbit? I took aim at him and tried it and he saw it coming and he kept going lower and lower until when I finally did figure I had him, I missed, fell down, and he went in and scored a goal! He's a freak."

Bill listened. He listened partly to the words, but partly to something that was more than words. It seemed obvious, whatever the reason, that Moore was declaring peace between them with this casual talk. He had a sort of humour in the way he talked now. For the first time Bill could understand why Pam could look upon him not as a public enemy, as most people who played against him did, but as a totally acceptable big brother.

"What does your father do?" Benny asked abruptly.

Bill told him.

"A professor!" Moore said. "And he lets you associate with the kind of goons that play hockey?"

"They aren't all goons," Bill said. "In fact, there aren't many goons."

"There aren't many goons," Moore mimicked, but his heart wasn't really in the mimicry, this time. "I was just quoting the way some guys in the papers write about games that I play in," he said. "A professor eh?" He paused. "Take my old man now – he drinks for a living. At least, that's what he does best. Not a bad guy, you know – or did you know? Did Pam tell you anything?"

"She didn't tell me," Bill said.

Moore got up and shook a long ash off his cigar. "Yep," he said. "He had a shoe store. I don't remember it. He'd lost it before I grew up enough to remember. But how does a guy get to be a drunk running a shoe store? You tell me. My grandma tells me that he didn't drink much before my mother died. I used to wonder why would he start to drink then, when he had two kids that he was supposed to look after by himself? But I stopped worrying about that. I see him once in a while."

Bill listened. There seemed nothing he could say that wouldn't be fatuous. He waited for Moore to go on, but Moore puffed out smoke and looked at the ceiling. One thing still bothered Bill. He didn't want to be nosey, but he wanted to know. "Pam told me about what happened at the swimming pool. Everything okay there?"

Moore swung his feet to the floor, staring at Bill. "She told you what?"

"She told me – everything," Bill said.

"What did the guy say about her?"

Bill said, "He called her a red-headed broad, and that if . . ."

"Okay!" Moore said. "I didn't think she'd tell anybody that. But I found out one thing." His voice had dropped a little and had lost a great deal of its bombast. "She went and told Pokesy Wares about it, too. And a lot of stuff about how I used to look after her when she was younger. . . ." Moore let out a long sigh and then grinned. "Must have been quite a tear-jerker. Pokesy has never been so nearly polite to me before in his life." And right there, Bill thought, might be the reason for all this change: he found out that somebody supported him – and that somebody else wanted to give him every chance.

There was another long pause. Moore got up and walked around the room. "She's a good kid," he said. "You know? She's only eighteen. If I'd had her sense at eighteen I'd be in this league by now, instead of with that suspension rap to beat before I can even play."

One thing had been worrying Bill every since he had seen the two men with Moore earlier in the day. He'd looked at them closely and thought of what Pam said, and what she had left unsaid, about their apartment and the fact that she didn't like going out with them. He hesitated. But then he spoke. This was going so well that he felt he could get it off his chest.

"Maybe it's none of my business," he began.

"Then don't say it," Moore said.

But Bill went on, ". . . but I'd think you'd want to keep her away from that fellow you were with today."

"Tom Amadio?"

Bill nodded.

"What do you know about him?" Moore asked, and there was a wary look in his eyes now.

"Just what Pam told me," Bill said. "That she doesn't want to go out with him."

Moore looked at Bill for a few seconds longer. "Yeah," he said finally. He dropped his eyes, then. "Well, nobody forces her to go out with him, eh?"

They went for walks, later. Moore went first. Bill went to the lobby and found Jim Butt and a few others there. He and Butt and Jiggs Maniscola and Anson Oakley went for a walk and watched a cabin cruiser going through the city's lift lock. It was quite an operation. Once the boat had entered the lock, the water poured in and lifted the cruiser up until it was high above the level of the water it had come from. Then gates opened and it sailed out to continue its journey. When they were walking back to the hotel, Bill suddenly laughed.

The others said, "What's funny?"

"McGarry," Bill said, still laughing. "He said that when you've seen one lift lock, you've seen 'em all!"

Moore was in bed when Bill got in, a little after ten. The light was out. Moore obviously wasn't taking any chances with the curfew tonight. Bill tiptoed around, although he didn't know for sure that Moore was asleep. When he got into bed himself he lay wide awake. Ordinarily he would read for a while, but perhaps this was just as well. This way, he'd be even more ready for tomorrow.

He was almost asleep when the phone rang.

"Benny?" a voice said.

Bill said, "I think he's asleep."

"Wake him."

Bill turned on the light. Moore's eyes were

wide open. Bill had the feeling that he hadn't been asleep at all. He took the phone and said hello, and listened.

"No," he said. "Don't be a fool. I'm not sore at the guy. Leave him alone."

When he hung up he picked up a pack of cigarettes and lit one before he turned out the light. "Those crazy guys," he said.

Bill rolled over and blinked at him and said, "What?"

Benny said, "That was Amadio. He said they were going to rough up that guy I tangled with at the swimming pool the other night. Can you imagine the jam that would get me into?"

There was another pause. "I'm through with them," Benny said, slowly and thoughtfully.

CHAPTER 15 ▬

A few days before, Tim Merrill had shoved under the glass on the dresser a single sheet of paper that looked like this:

TORONTO MAPLE LEAFS EXHIBITION SCHEDULE

	vs.	at
September 18	Chicago	St. Catharines
September 21	St. Catharines	Peterborough
September 23	Rangers	Kitchener
September 25	Chicago	Toronto
September 27	Winnipeg	Winnipeg
September 28	Montreal	Toronto
September 29	Vancouver	Vancouver
September 30	Edmonton	Edmonton
October 2	Buffalo	Toronto

Bill often had looked at the schedule in the first week of training. Tim left it when he moved down the hall with the general change on Sunday. At 6:45 on Monday morning with another clear-skied dawn outside he looked at it again while he waited for Moore to get out of the shower.

Benny came out, dripping all over the rug, rubbing himself with a towel.

"What are you doing up so early?" Bill said. "You're not on the ice until nine, are you?"

"Things to do," Benny said. "The coach asked me to see him at breakfast. He eats with you guys." He rubbed the towel over his shoulders and down the big muscular body and finally was bending over, drying his feet, when he said without looking up, "He was trying to get the league president on the phone last night to see that I'd be allowed to play in this exhibition tomorrow night."

"I hope you make it," Bill said, from the bathroom doorway.

When he looked back, Moore was grinning. "Yeah! We got our little show to put on for the people, eh?" He was still looking straight at Bill and smiling. He wasn't an easy guy to figure out.

The day went fairly fast. Bill enjoyed the walks to and from the rink now. The clear crispness of the morning air would give way to a warming sun by the time he walked back. And he was beginning to get accustomed to the fact that this one spot in the dressing room was his and his alone: Spunska's place. When he thought of that, he thought: Some year it'll be my place through the whole training and then on into the Leaf room in Toronto. But sometimes he would look across the room to someone else, someone a few years older who must have been good when he was eighteen, too. Must have been ambitious. And still was – and yet never made it to the Leafs. Or he'd look at Buff Koska, the fretwork of stitches across his gnarled face, and think: He knows more about playing defence than I can learn in years, but maybe he's not good enough for the Leafs any more. And then he would think of the teachers who told him that he shouldn't stake too much on skill that was entirely physical, for physical skills could be lost through injury and age and then what was left?

That morning after the first shift, Bill sat in the stands for a while with some other players. He liked watching Benny Moore. He broke like a racehorse from a starting gate – he could stop, change direction, slip off a check, hand out a check. Watching, fifteen hundred miles from home, he got thinking back to when he had started skating himself – going to the old rink early every morning all by himself and trying to learn how to skate.

Then one morning Pete Gordon had turned up. Pete had been the star player on the Daniel Mac team in Winnipeg and had been moved that year to this new school, Northwest, not because his family had moved, but just because of a change in school boundaries. Bill hardly knew him then, but Pete had been going through an argument with himself. All his friends and fellow players were still at Daniel Mac and he just couldn't bring himself to turn out for Northwest, a new school, new team. He told Bill later that one of the things that got him moving in the right direction was when he heard that Spunska, this Polish kid who couldn't even skate, was going down to the rink every morning and trying.

Pete was a small, fair-haired boy, a centre. "I just got to thinking about how much I had to be thankful for and what a jerk I was being," he told Bill later. Bill had understood what he meant. He thought of it now. Sometimes people with talent never do learn until someone who hasn't much talent climbs slowly by, on hard work alone. Later Bill had been allowed as an extra body for practice scrimmages. Now he remembered that tiny dressing room, the guys bringing in their big duffel bags with their hockey equipment. Half of it still would be damp from the last time they'd used it. They'd dump it along the floor and climb into soggy underwear, grousing at themselves for not having had enough sense to hang it up.

On the ice, Bad Benny Moore, his roommate, had just scored a goal.

Bill cheered, "Hey, Benny!"

Up among the scouts, Squib Jackson noticed.

Funny the way it struck Squib: sitting up there with a few scouts, for some reason he had just been thinking of a story he'd read in Lee Vincent's column last year about how that fair-haired centre, what was his name? – Pete Gordon, that was it! – had gone down early in the mornings and found nailkegs set in a crazy pattern for Spunska to skate between, to see if he could do it without knocking them down. Squib always had liked that story. One kid helping another. As he thought that, Benny had got his goal on a hard slapper from the blueline.

And he'd heard Spunska's booming yell, "Hey, Benny!"

He'd looked up to see Spunska standing up. And he'd wondered: Pete Gordon and Spunska. Bill Spunska and Benny Moore. Could be.

Along the row of seats Pokesy was making notes. Squib said, "What about Moore's suspension?"

"It's called off," Pokesy said. "The kid's on his own. I told him before you were up – and you call yourself a scout! What do you think he's scoring goals for down there?" Then he was serious. "I'll tell you, I never saw a happier guy," he said. "If he's all straightened out, how can we keep him off the Leafs?"

CHAPTER 16 ▬

Tuesday night, it seemed strange to be going to play hockey. The temperature had gone into the eighties during the day. The parking lots were beginning to fill at a quarter to seven when Bill and McGarry and Butt arrived at the rink and were held up outside in the dozens of youngsters and some adults, too, collecting autographs. Some of the kids, Bill noticed, would stare at him hard and long and then would shove an autograph book in front of him. When he had signed it, they'd turn the book around quickly to see who he was. Seemed crazy, to him, getting an autograph from someone whose name they didn't even know.

But some knew him, too.

One woman who looked old enough to be his mother, but had a kind of wild look about her, an over-excitement, leaned close to him and said, "Murder that Moore for me, sonny boy!"

"Why?" Bill said, startled.

"Ah-h-h-h," she said, as if he were trying to fool her. "I've read all about it. I watched him here last year and our own team or not, I didn't like the man, and that's the truth."

But then she dashed away from him to get another autograph and back there fifty feet or so he saw Moore moving through the crowd. He'd heard about how Moore got on the night of a game. That intent look that he had in practices was there. He scarcely seemed to see the people crowding around him. He'd stop and sign only when someone planted himself firmly in his way and refused to move.

In the warm-up, Bill heard a girl's voice call, "Bill!" He looked around for the other Bills on the team. Leafs were practising shooting on Johnny Bosfield and the minor leaguers at the other end were peppering Ed Hill. The seats were almost full. "Bill!" the call came again. "Bill Spunska!"

Then he saw Pam. She was sitting in a rail seat near centre ice. He glanced toward the workout. He wasn't sure that he should be leaving, but he noticed that two or three of the Leafs were leaning on the rail, and some of the St. Catharines players, too, talking to people. He skated over. He never attempted to fool himself about the warm feeling he got when she was around. She was some girl. Tonight she was wearing a short leather coat and her eyes were sparkling with the excitement. She turned to a pleasant-looking older woman as Bill came up.

"Hi!" she said. "This is Bill, Mrs. Koska."

Mrs. Koska smiled. "I've met your mother in Winnipeg. We go to the same church, did you know?"

He didn't. He'd known Buff Koska came from Winnipeg, but he'd never seen him out there.

She was smiling again. "When Buff is ready to quit, maybe you'll be ready to take his place," she said. "Have to keep a Pole on the Leafs somehow, you know!"

Pam said, "Just wanted you to know where we're sitting. So you won't knock anybody into our laps. Especially Benny, now!"

"I won't," Bill promised.

"A few of the wives have plans for later," Mrs. Koska said. "Would you come?"

"Well, uh," said Bill, looking at Pam. She nodded. Suddenly he felt very good indeed. "Sure!" he said. He skated back to the workout. The puck came out to him and he caught it just right and drove it back hard at Bosfield, who said mildly, "Take it easy, kid. Save it for the enemy."

When the game began, the rink was full. Bill often thought back afterward to the elation he'd felt before this game. A game coming up. A date with Pam for after. Going out to eat with the other Leafs and their wives.

And then there was the excitement of the

bench, with Pokesy pacing behind, sometimes yelling jibes at Percy Simpson behind the other bench. Since Simpson worked under Wares in the Leafs' system, this was a rivalry of a different sort. Many of the players had been brought along through the Leafs' system together, had roomed together, played together, fought hard for wins together against other teams. Now the St. Catharines players were out to prove that they belonged on the Leafs. And the Leafs were out to prove that there wasn't room for any more players with the Leafs, no matter how good they were.

And then up in the crowd, for the first time, a cry: "We want Spunska! We want Moore!"

Pokesy, standing behind Bill, muttered: "Somebody here can read, anyway."

Both teams were using six defencemen. Three pairs. The coaches started out changing defences on every line change. The first time that Moore came out, Bill wasn't on the ice. But later in the period Pokesy began experimenting a little, looking for goals, trying to get his big line away from St. Catharines' most dogged checking line.

The first time Bill and Moore were out together they never came even close to one another, each busy at his own tasks.

Bill forgot the so-called feud. To him it was over – so what the heck? The crowd would re-

174

mind him sometimes, when Moore picked up the puck and rushed his way, or Bill went toward him. But Bill gradually sank into the game completely himself, forgetting the crowd, forgetting that Pam Moore was just a few yards along the rail, forgetting everything but the man coming in, the cut of skates, the whack of sticks and bodies, the fierce competition for a puck in the corner, the necessity of keeping a man off balance when he got parked in front of your net and someone had the puck and was trying to get it out for a shot on goal.

First period over. Intermission. They sucked on half oranges, relaxed. Out again. Once Moore knocked him down cleanly. Once he poked the puck away from Moore.

And then, with the clock showing 9:20 in the second period, Bill came out from behind the net with the puck and saw no one handy to take a pass. Otto Tihane, circling in front of the net, yelled, "Go, kid!"

As Bill came up the right side, through his own zone, something came into his mind. Moore was playing left defence up ahead. Bill had made another couple of rushes in that direction earlier in the game. Both times Moore had skated him off into the boards. This time he wondered fleetingly if Moore would be looking again for that attempt to crash through along the boards. Could be.

Bill's old system in carrying the puck had been to go straight down the middle. The surprise value of that bull-like rush had been lost after the first day. He'd recognized that, after landing on the seat of his pants more times than he could remember. Now every defenceman in the camp knew that he had to be well braced when Spunska came down the middle and they would be waiting for him. Bill was still no Fancy Dan on skates and everyone knew that, too.

A back-checking forward swung at the puck but Bill pulled it out of his way and kept going. The forward peeled off to cover his check. Now in the centre zone Bill was thinking, I'll try it anyway. If it worked, fine. If it didn't, well, at least he wouldn't be crashed into the boards again. Maybe into the ice, but not into the boards.

Suddenly Bill turned on the steam. He skated hard for the hole between Moore and the boards. This gap was about twelve feet wide right then, with Moore closing it warily, half turning, ready to go with him, stick out, and Bill skating for that hole as if his life depended on getting there. When Jim Butt saw what he was doing he backed up suddenly, keeping his check with him, leaving a little room. Then Butt crossed behind Bill, ready to drive for the front of the net where he might take a pass or pick up a rebound. But when Bill saw Moore committing himself for that last few feet of closing up the gap between him and the boards, suddenly he jammed his right foot into the ice and changed direction.

Crash! Moore's body went into the boards, missing the empty air where Bill would have been. And there was Bill turning slightly and with the ice like a broad and empty highway between him and the goal. He heard the crowd's roars. He must have heard because he remembered later. Buff Koska, Moore's defence partner, had been watching the play alertly. He started across to intercept. But all this was in a split second. Butt, crossing behind Bill and driving in over the blueline, brushed against Koska just enough to throw him off stride. Then Butt's check got to him – put his stick across Butt's and pinned it to the ice.

Then it was just Bill and Ed Hill, the goalkeeper. Bill leaned into the shot. This was the way he had leaned into shot after shot for hours every day for months back in the old rink at home in Winnipeg. His arms came through, his wrists rolled, and he drove a shot about six inches off the ice to the stick side of the goalkeeper and it was in. And then he was making a big swoop through the face-off circle, his arms raised delightedly, while Moore was still picking himself up off the ice fruitlessly on the other side.

Up in the stands, the delight was unconfined. Unrefined, too, for that matter. People jeered at Moore, as he skated across the ice toward Bill. Bill saw him coming and wondered, looking at Moore's red face and blazing eyes, but he slowed down and waited.

Down behind the bench Pokesy Wares had shoved his hat over his eyes and was walking back and forth, clapping his hands. Along the rail, Pam Moore was moaning, "Oh, I don't know whether to cheer for Bill or feel sorry for Benny. . . ." And then she, too, watched.

No one in the crowd knew what was said when Moore reached Bill, but they yelled for blood. No one knew but Moore and Bill. Bill was ready for anything, except what came. "You sure fooled me, kid," Moore said.

"I was lucky," Bill said. "I just thought . . ."

The linesmen had skated over alertly in case there was going to be trouble. Then they stood there grinning. And seeing them grin made some people in the stands jeer. But Pokesy Wares, Squib Jackson, and Pam Moore relaxed and smiled, too.

"You just thought . . ." Moore mimicked. "You just thought you could suck me into closing you off – and you did!"

Bill thought the moment had come when he might even try a little kidding. "Better luck next time," he said politely. And Moore made a little motion with his stick, a small threatening motion. He said later it was the first time in his life that he had made that little motion with his stick and had not meant it.

The goal stood up for a while. Second period over. Intermission again. Then in the third the teams traded goals, twice. 2-0. Then 2-1. 3-1. Then 3-2. And it was almost at the end of the game, the last minute, when it happened.

Simpson had taken out his goalkeeper, to put out an extra forward. Under normal circumstances, Pokesy would have put out his oldest and most experienced players. This time he left Bill out there.

Otto Tihane skated to the bench to question him about it.

Wares barked, "I can look at you old goats all season long! I know what you can do!" And then, as if in a further gesture of defiance, he sent Jim Butt over the boards. It was with twenty-five seconds to go, a face-off in the Leafs' end, that the play began.

The face-off was in the circle to the right of Johnny Bosfield. Otto Tihane set his big jaw and looked over the six opposition players lined up inside the blueline. He knew the system for this play. Heck, they all trained for it, through the Leafs' system. The opposing wings were one on each side of the face-off circle. Buff Koska and Benny Moore were covering the points at the blueline. The extra man was Bones Raymond. He was high between the face-off circles, in the slot directly in front of the goal.

Leaf wings were ready to cover the St. Catharines wings, Otto would take the face-off. That left two men to spurt out and cover the three remaining St. Catharines players as soon as the puck was dropped.

Tihane skated over to Bill. "You go for Koska out on the far point." Then he said to Butt, "You get Bones Raymond there, behind the circle. If the puck goes to Moore, cover him."

Then he went back to the circle again. He knew that if the St. Catharines centre got the face-off, he'd try to get it back to the slot man, Raymond. If Butt got to Raymond fast enough, he'd pass back either to Benny Moore on one point or across the ice to Koska on the other. Otto figured Butt could barge on past Raymond and try for Moore, but somebody had to be going for Koska.

The crowd roared for a while, settled down, and then began to shout for action. Ott Tihane moved in, skates set wide, ready for the drop of the puck.

Down it came! He lunged forward to tie up the other centre, trying to kick the puck back. His foot missed. Bill sped toward Koska and Butt toward Raymond. Maniscola swept in to pick it up. His check knocked him down. A St.

Catharines player whacked the puck. Another St. Catharines player was wheeling to get away from his check. The blade of his stick hit Bill on the cheek. He reeled, then kept on doggedly, trying to get his direction and legs again. The puck bounced out to Bones Raymond. Raymond saw Butt coming and couldn't see Moore so he passed across to Koska, who seemed clear. At the last second Butt reached out his long arms and deflected the pass just as it left Raymond's stick. Bill was close when he saw Koska set to take a pass and then suddenly trying to turn. And Bill saw the puck flying out into the centre zone. Beyond it was the open net at the other end.

Bill changed direction. Koska tried to check him but couldn't reach. The puck was right ahead, sliding toward centre.

It was a sixth sense rather than anything he could see that informed him that he was in danger, just as he was reaching for the puck.

The boards were alongside on his left, the puck was there, his stick was out for it, the crowd's roar was deafening all around him, when he sensed, or heard, or felt, someone hurtling toward him.

There was a wild yell of "Look out!" With his stick on the puck, Bill made his move instinctively – a fierce, quick lowering of his shoulder and a springing check to knock down the man trying to check him, twisting, fighting with legs and shoulders and arms and stick to keep balance. Suddenly Bill saw that it was Moore, whose helmet flew off and who hit the ice with his head and collapsed limply there and lay still.

Bill dropped his stick and gloves and knelt beside him, saying, "Benny! Benny!"

Suddenly all was hush and every voice an echo. There was a scream. Moore was crumpled on the ice beside the boards. Bobby Deyell was slipping and sliding out across the ice. It was like a bad dream: the stretcher coming, Moore being lifted gently on, his face so white where it had been full of high colour before. Bill went to the bench. Bobby Deyell was saying a few quiet words to Pokesy Wares and then the coach was saying, "Call the ambulance first."

They played the last few seconds of the game. The crowd, some much subdued but others chattering with excitement, began to move.

The stretcher with Moore on it was being manoeuvred slowly toward the rink entrance. The players left the ice. Bill had to wait for an opening in the crowd to make his way to the dressing room. Several players made a point of tapping him on the seat of his pants with their sticks. Some said, "Don't let it get you, kid." And, "These things happen."

But high in the crowd a voice called, "Well, I

guess you win that round, Spunska." Followed by laughter.

And then, finally, Bill was in the dressing room corridor, feeling stunned.

"What happened?" Wares said. "I couldn't see."

Bill said, "Just at the last second I could see somebody coming, and I checked him. . . . I didn't even know it was Benny . . ."

CHAPTER 17 ▬

"How did it happen?"

Red Barrett of the *Star* asked the question, the next time. The dressing room seemed full of newspapermen. They were all around Bill. One was Dan Sokorny of the Toronto *Sun*, another Mike Bradley of the *Globe and Mail*. There were six or seven others. A radio sports reporter from Toronto introduced himself. The sports editor of the Peterborough *Examiner* was there. It was about twenty minutes since Moore had been wheeled out on a stretcher to the ambulance, still unconscious. Most of the other fellows in the dressing room had dressed quickly. Bill remembered the wives waiting. He'd been supposed to go, too. He thought of Pam and felt sick. But when he'd come out of the shower the reporters had been waiting with their insistent questions.

Bill, answering Red Barrett, was beginning to feel like a record, playing over and over. "I was going for the puck along the boards. Just at the last instant I had a feeling that somebody was coming at me from the side. I don't know whether I looked back or whether I just got it out of the corner of my eye but I just saw this uniform coming at me. I put my shoulder down and lunged out to keep him away. I was still going for the puck to try to make the play on the open net. But the check . . . I did throw the check."

Barrett said, "The way I saw it from the stands, you were going for the puck and Moore was going either for you or for the puck, it was hard to say from where I was sitting, but then I thought you saw him coming and sort of launched yourself at him while you were still reaching for the puck. So that agrees, all right, eh?"

Bill nodded.

Otto Tihane had been sitting listening. He was fully dressed. Normally he would have left. But he had hung around and now he spoke casually.

"I was on the ice not very far away from it. It was strictly an accident. I don't think it would be right to call it anything else. Especially after all the publicity these two kids have got." He looked around all the faces. "I think it was just a collision and that's that. Moore might have been going for the puck or he might have been going to cream Spunska along the boards – nobody will know that until he comes to."

"If he comes to," said a voice. It was the man from the Toronto radio station. He was stocky, with bulging eyes and a deep, resonant voice. Bill couldn't remember his name.

"How many times would you say you and Moore have tangled since this camp opened?" he asked.

Bill looked up at him rather in surprise and said, "Gosh, I couldn't even guess. I mean, in scrimmages you might run into a fellow half a dozen times and not even be sure who it was."

The radio man insisted, "I mean the sort of collision you would remember."

Bill thought for a minute. Before he could speak, Tihane interrupted. "What's that got to do with it?" he asked.

Red Barrett said, "Take it easy, Otto. It's a fair enough question."

"Fair question, my eye!" Tihane said. "You start throwing loaded questions at a kid like this, and I know what comes out the other end – enough to hang the guy."

"Look . . ." the radio man began.

"Look!" Tihane said. "What do you want out of the kid, anyway? He told you he was going for the puck and somebody came at him from the side and he wasn't even sure who it was. So what's he going to do? Let himself get creamed into the boards? Now what do you think he's going to say? Tell you that he rigged it so that

Moore would hit the ice and fracture his skull? What are you, a nut or something?"

The radio man had gone white during this tirade. He did not answer Tihane but said to Bill, "You and Moore have been feuding ever since the camp opened. Right?"

Bill said, "I guess so."

"You've knocked each other down at least half a dozen times. In fact, every time one of you got the puck and went in on the other somebody went down. Right?"

Bill nodded.

"So today the puck was free and you both were going for it, you tangled, and Moore came out of it with a head injury. Right?"

"Right," Bill said, feeling numb and rather sick at this way of putting it.

"When you got the goal by beating him, and he came and spoke to you, what did he say?"

Bill told him and saw the growing disbelief in the man's eyes. The man laughed. "He told you you'd sure fooled him!" he said. "Then what did he raise his stick for, as if he was going to hit you?"

"He was just kidding," Bill said.

"Benny Moore, kidding!" the man said, and turned to the audience of other reporters, waiting for the laugh. Some smiled. Others looked as if they didn't like the way this line of questioning was going at all.

Tihane said quietly, "You're the Bad Benny Moore of radioland, I guess."

The man flushed. Then Barrett spoke. Of all the sportswriters, Red was the one that had been around hockey the longest. "You should remember, though, that this kid hasn't been the aggressor in any of the incidents between the two," he said to the radio man. "He's had a real good training camp without any assist from Bad Benny Moore. Also, you haven't been here for the last week like the rest of us have. . . ." There was just a hint of irony in his tone. "So maybe you won't mind me telling you that there's never been a hint of temper in the way this kid has played. He's played it hard, but there's been nothing nasty about him."

The radio man made a couple of notes. But even Barrett's soothing words couldn't put out of Bill's mind the driving tone of the questions earlier.

In a few minutes they left. Tihane and Bill and Bobby Deyell were the only three that were left in the dressing room now. Deyell wore his usual brisk, jovial manner. He seemed to talk more loudly when he was trying to cheer somebody up. "Come on, kid," he said. "That might have been you carried out of here, or it might have been Tihane or it might have been anybody. This is a man's game. Forget it. Don't let it bother you."

Bill kept on dressing. It seemed to him that for the last half hour, he'd been numb. Now he was gradually beginning to come out of it and feel the pain.

The worst thing was, and this flicked across his mind like a knife, had he tried to hurt Moore? He had told those men that he hadn't been sure it was Moore; that he'd just known it was somebody coming at him. But he'd have to know it was Moore! There wasn't anybody else on the team who would have come at him in just that way. This was the first time in Bill's life that it occurred to him that there might be more to a man's action than appeared even on the surface of his own mind.

He was tying the laces of his shoes when Tihane said, "Coming out to eat?"

Bill said, "No."

"Come on."

It wasn't a plea. It was an order. Bill got up and followed. They met Buff Koska coming back down the corridor. He stopped when he saw Bill and Tihane coming. "I was sent to get you," he said.

Outside the rink, the little group of players and wives was waiting in the soft autumn evening. There was a bit of smell of burning leaves in the air, and the acrid smell that goes with fall sometimes. At first Bill couldn't see exactly who was in the group. But then he saw that Pam was not. Neither was Mrs. Koska. "They took my car and went to the hospital," Koska said. In the dim light Bill could see the questioning look in his eyes, a question as to how he was taking all this. How was he? Well, he'd been almost afraid to see Pam. But now it was worse. He didn't know what she thought. . . .

"I'm sorry about Benny," he said miserably.

"We know you are," Koska said.

"Do you know how he is?"

"I've called the hospital," he said. "I'm to call back in an hour. You come with us."

"I'd rather not," Bill said.

Ott Tihane, he now realized, hadn't been more than three feet from his side ever since this happened. He was there now. "You come with us."

Again it was in order.

That night, alone in the room, Bill phoned the hospital several times and got no new information. Then Bobby Deyell phoned him. "Pokesy asked me to call you," he said. "Benny hasn't come out of it. There seems to be some pressure on the brain and they're going to operate."

Bill tried to phone Pam later but she wasn't in her room. Still later, alone, he was sick.

CHAPTER 18 ▬

"Look!" Pam argued. "I saw it happen! I don't blame you. Benny would be the last to blame you. It wasn't a dirty play!"

Bill turned away from the hotel desk. It was seven in the morning. Pam didn't start this early. She had come down especially to see Bill. The word from the hospital was that Benny was still unconscious.

Pam walked away from the desk with Bill. He had to go to breakfast, if he could eat. All night there had been that sound in his ears of Benny's head hitting the ice as he spun forward and down. "I didn't try to hurt him," Bill said.

"I know! I knew at the time! Bill . . ."

He stopped at the archway. Other players went on in to breakfast. She waited until they were briefly alone again, and she pleaded with her eyes. "I don't know quite how to say it," she said. "But . . . don't let it hurt you. I mean, hurt the way you play the game or . . ." She let it finish there.

"Okay," Bill said. For the instant, he meant

it. When he turned, he felt better again. Five seconds later he heard that sound in his mind again, of Benny's head striking the ice.

"Look," said Squib Jackson. This was at breakfast. The chief scout hadn't been up this early all week. Like Pam Moore, he'd come down early – on purpose. "Look," he said. "I know you feel bad. I'm going to make you feel worse."

Bill looked at him sharply.

"The publicity on that feud between you and Moore was too big. All over the country, sports editors are going to pick up the news this morning and they're going to write columns referring to the feud. They won't have seen the play, but they'll interpret it. They'll say it was part of the feud and that you've sure won this round. And people will write letters to the editor and denounce hockey as a blood sport, turning young Canadians into hooligans. Etcetera. Etcetera. You ready for that?"

Bill just stared at him. He'd seen this sort of thing happen to other players, after fights or accidents in the game. But to him? Would the people in Winnipeg believe it? "What should I do?" Bill asked.

"Keep quiet, mostly. Answer any questions honestly. Don't get mad. Just keep thinking of one thing: Benny Moore is too tough a kid to blame you. Remember that. In a few days it'll be all right."

Bill gazed down into his plate and pushed his food around with his fork. "It'll be all right if Benny Moore is all right," he said.

Squib Jackson said nothing to that.

The trouble was, Bill thought, nothing is quite as clear cut as the simple words, "It was an accident." Or even, "It was not an accident."

At the workout, he felt dead.

"Come on, Spunska, keep your eyes open!" the coach said once after a whistle and a change of players. Bill smarted in sudden surprise.

Jiggs Maniscola and Otto Tihane heard what the coach said. They sat with Bill on the bench.

Maniscola said, "Don't let it worry you. He should take it a little easier on you today."

Tihane said, "Take it easier? Why?"

Maniscola looked at him in surprise. "That business yesterday! Spunska comes out here today, he's got more on his mind than the rest of us."

Tihane was watching the play on the ice. "Baloney!" he said. At the other blueline, Buff Koska caught Ron Stephens with his shoulder. Stephens landed with a thud on the seat of his pants.

Tihane said, "Do you think if you had got hurt instead of Moore in that check – and that's the kind of check that the puck carrier is more likely to get hurt in – that Moore would be sitting here now feeling sorry for himself? Not a bit of it. He would be sorry that he had hurt you. But he'd know that he'd meant to stop you, but not hurt you – and he'd know it might be him next time."

There was a pile-up on the boards right in front of them. Buff Koska and Steve Baldur had been chasing a loose puck. Jim Butt came in from the side and tried to snake it away. The three of them crashed into the boards, sticks whacking, skates cutting. Their grunts could be heard in the empty rink, along with the coach yelling, "Get it the so-and-so out of there and get moving."

"I was just a little kid," Tihane said, "when Ted Kennedy checked Gordie Howe that time in Detroit. I read about it later. Howe wound up with a fractured skull, in hospital. They flew his mother and father down from Saskatchewan. For a day or two you'd have thought those Detroit newspapers were running a lynch mob. And this was in a playoff, remember. And Kennedy had to skate onto that ice two days later not knowing if some crazy character was going to try to shoot him from the stands or some crazy woman was going to hit him over the head with a handbag loaded with face cream jars, or what."

194

Bill couldn't help grinning. The face cream jars in the handbag did it. He stopped just as quickly.

"And I'll tell you one reason why nothing happened to Ted Kennedy in that game," Tihane said. "At least nothing that was going to hurt him permanently. It was because every guy on both teams knew that every time two fellows go into the boards together there's a chance that somebody's going to get hurt. Many years later somebody was interviewing Gord Howe on television and they got talking about the rough aspects of the game and how they could be changed. Howe made what I thought was the definitive comment about professional hockey. He said, 'I like it the way it is. Sure, it's sometimes tough, but why not? It's a man's game.' "

Tihane looked at the other two. "Remember that," he said. "I might get hurt, you might get hurt, anybody might get hurt. You've got to understand *that* before you can be any good at this game at all."

Behind them, there'd been a clumping of skates. They'd been so engrossed in what Tihane was saying that no one looked up.

"If you had let me know that you were going to be preaching, Ott," Merv McGarry said, "I would have made sure that the organist was here to provide appropriate background music."

Tihane thoughtfully turned with his stick in his right hand and swung it hard about six inches off the floor. McGarry took off in a ballet leap, the stick swishing by under his skates. Then he ran along the rubber matting to get out of the way, shouting imprecations.

After that morning workout, Bill slipped out, alone. Tihane had helped some. He recognized the logic but he couldn't make his emotions recognize it. After the afternoon workout he walked a long way. He wished he could talk this thing over with his dad. In matters of ethics, to Bill the final authority was his father. And this was a matter of ethics. Despite the fact that he was sure that the manner in which he had attempted to beat Moore's check had been unconscious reflex, he still couldn't rid himself of the idea that somehow he was guilty.

At five o'clock he walked up the road to the hospital. He did then what he sometimes had done as a child in times of stress. Without stopping walking, he closed his eyes. "Please God, help him," he said. He opened his eyes and walked on feeling a little better.

At the hospital information desk, the woman looked at him a little curiously. "The club doctor just went up about half an hour ago," she said. "You could go to the fourth floor and look around for him. Ask the nurse up there."

The long, quiet, tile corridors had a stillness

about them that he found disquieting. On the elevator, an orderly wheeled in a woman on a stretcher, a woman with a tired, pain-wracked face and her hair all straggly on the pillow beside her. Bill noticed that she must be normally a pretty woman.

At the fourth floor he got out. He was facing a small office in which two or three nurses worked. He asked one if Dr. Murphy was around. The nurse, scarcely looking at him, said, "He's busy right now. There's a waiting room at the end of the hall. I'll send him down when he comes out."

Bill walked along the hall on the balls of his feet, keeping his clicking heels off the floors for quiet. As he passed the long rows of doors, he wondered which one was Benny's.

The waiting room faced out over the city. It was furnished with Danish chairs and coffee tables. Standing facing out of one of the windows were two men. Both were smoking. They both turned when Bill entered. They were the ones who'd been with Moore on Sunday going into the elevator. "Well, well," one of them said. "The kid from Winnipeg."

All that Bill had been thinking, piling up the possible blame against himself, came to the top of his mind now. He made as if to turn and leave. One of them jumped forward a couple of steps and said, "Hey!"

Bill turned again. Close up, the two looked somewhat alike. One was two or three inches taller than the other. "We were going to come around looking for you," the taller one said. His voice had a flat quality that seemed vaguely menacing.

"It was an accident, wasn't it?" the shorter one said.

Bill nodded and said slowly, "Yes."

The shorter one said, "We didn't think a young guy like you would do something like that on purpose."

"Why were you going to come around looking for me, then?" Bill asked curiously.

The shorter one was Amadio, the one who had tried to date Pam. "We just got the idea that you misunderstood us," he said. "I mean, just because we were friends of Benny's didn't mean we couldn't be friends of yours, too."

"Friends of mine?" Bill said, baffled.

"We know a lot of the players," the tall one said, expansively.

"Sure!" said Amadio. "Not only on this club but all over the league – guys who played here when they were juniors, and we could do things for. Like get them into places in Toronto and other cities where we have friends. Why, down in Florida when the season was over last spring we had three or four guys come and stay with us, near Daytona. . . . Had a ball."

There was a step behind Bill. He saw their expressions change. Still smiling, now, but wary. Bill turned. Dr. Murphy was standing in the doorway. "What are you doing here?" he asked Bill sharply.

"I thought I'd . . . come and see how Benny was."

The doctor glanced at the other two and then at Bill. "He's still the same. I think the operation worked – as far as we can tell now. The skull fracture is one thing, any damage to the brain another. He hasn't come to, yet. Now you go back to the hotel. And stay away from these two. Between them they've been about three-quarters of Benny's trouble."

Amadio took a quick puff from a cigarette and said flatly, "You know it all, eh, Doc?"

"I know quite a bit more than you think I do," the doctor said. "I can warn you right now that Pokesy Wares knows quite a bit more than you think he does, too. And that Benny Moore was warned about you two by Pokesy, two days before he was hurt."

Bill was trying to take this in. "Warned about them?" he said. "He said the other night that he was through with them, but he didn't say anything more . . ."

"Well, I'll tell you what he knew," the doctor said, gazing directly at the two men. "Just so we'll all know. When Pokesy was talking to the league office about Benny being reinstated for these exhibition games, they told Pokesy that there was one more thing Benny should be warned about and it might as well be now. . . . His associations."

Bill looked at Amadio. Suddenly both men looked startled and defensive.

"The league office said it had found out that you two had a place down in Florida last spring and you invited some young players down there and some NHLers, too," the doctor said. "One of the NHL players informed the league – a guy who knows that you make your living gambling, and are always hanging around NHL players trying to pick up inside information on injuries and things."

"So what?" said Amadio. "We're fans! So we bet? Who doesn't, one time or another . . ."

"Let's leave it this way," the doctor said. "As of now, your names have been given to every club in the NHL along with a request that players be warned now that any future association with you two will be regarded by the league president as suspicious."

The two men exchanged a glance. Amadio looked as if about to speak, but eventually muttered only, "Aw – we just came to see how he was." He butted his cigarette.

"So long," the doctor said. It was more of an

order than a farewell. They took the hint and left.

"What were they saying to you?" the doctor asked Bill.

"That they wanted to be friends," Bill said. "They mentioned the place in Florida. And that they had friends on a lot of clubs."

"Who'll turn and go the other way when they see 'em coming now," the doctor said. Then he smiled and put a hand on Bill's shoulder and started him along the hall. "No harm in your learning early," he said kindly, and then chuckled. "You know, Bill, maybe you've arrived – when a couple of hoods like those decide you're worth cultivating!"

"Could I go in and see him?" Bill asked suddenly.

"Benny?" the doctor said.

"Yes."

The doctor shook his head. "Bill," he said, "he's just lying there, unconscious, his head one big bandage, his eyes closed. It wouldn't do you or him any good at all."

CHAPTER 19 ▬

Jim Butt was waiting at the hotel, his long form covering two chairs. There was a little time before dinner, so Bill sat. The afternoon papers were in. They described the incident fairly closely, but hedged a little. "No one can say for sure how it happened until Benny Moore comes to," one paper said. A story from Montreal said that the league president was going to investigate, but hadn't yet received the referee's report.

"Let's eat," Jim said, rising.

"I don't know how I can eat," Bill said gloomily.

Jim said, grinning: "You get a fork, see, and you load it. Then you lift it toward your mouth, and open your mouth, and . . ."

"Ah-h-h," Bill said. "Enough!" He compressed his lips and shook his head. Darn it, he had to take it himself, like Benny was taking it himself. But what if this ruined his whole career? And then the thought: Whose career? Mine? Or Benny's? Who's worse off?

When they went into the dining room about half the players were there in the usual hum of conversation. Bill and Jim lined up at the buffet table. Cold meats, hot dishes, and salads were spread out. One of the ladies behind the counter took a plate and started to fill it for him.

While she worked, she made conversation. "Isn't it too bad about the accident to that nice Mr. Moore!" she said.

The other lady handling salads and desserts just about dropped the bowl of blueberries. "That nice Mr. Moore!" she exclaimed. "That isn't what you called him here two days ago when he took that whole pie on you, and you nearly out of that kind of pie!"

The first lady's face was comical in reply: "*That* was Mr. Moore?" she said. "*That* one! I tell you now, I didn't really know which one it was when I heard one named Moore got hurt, but they're all such fine boys I thought it was safe to say. . . ." She shook her head. "That one!" she said. And then defiantly, "I'm still sorry!"

Merv McGarry was right behind Bill in the line. He had heard all this. "If you thought Mr. Moore was nice, you probably got him mixed up with me," he said.

She started to smile, then saw who was speaking. "You! And you're another!"

"Ah, come now," McGarry said. "You're just saying that because you just don't want to embarrass me by saying in front of these people how much you like me."

The lady behind the table gave a mighty sniff.

When they sat down, Butt took a look at Bill's loaded plate. "I thought you said you weren't hungry," he said, with a chuckle.

Bill looked at it. "I guess that lady up there figured I needed something to keep my spirits up," he said.

He started by poking at the food listlessly. He finished by eating every scrap. He really didn't want to be hungry, but he was. Strange. And he kept on watching the clock on the wall.

Butt noticed. "What's up?"

"Hanson Blake comes on pretty soon," Bill said. "He hasn't been on since last night when he asked me all those questions." He'd found out the radio man's name today.

McGarry was across the table. "He got thrown out of our dressing room once."

"When was that?" Bill asked.

"One time some Philadelphia guy got hit in the face with a puck," McGarry said. "They were beating us, and I think it was Oakley, yes, it was Oakley – he was just a rookie then – he was clearing it out of our own end. He and the other guy had tangled about two or three times earlier in the game. Oakley shot it out and hit the guy right in the face! All the Philly guys said he had done it on purpose. You should have heard that Bobby Clarke on the bench. I think if he'd had a gun he'd have shot at Oakley. And all the time, of course, if Oakley could shoot so accurately that he could hit a guy in the face from a distance of about thirty feet, he'd score a hundred goals in a season. Nobody ever thought of that."

Bill asked, "But where did Blake come in?"

"He came into the dressing room after the game, with the rest of the guys, you know how they do. Hang around looking silly waiting for us to say something smart." McGarry glanced over at the table where the newspapermen were sitting. They apparently had not heard him, as there was no reaction. McGarry said in a louder voice, "You know how those media guys are after a game, they come with their tape recorders and notebooks and pencils and hang around looking silly waiting for us to say something smart. And then they steal it and put it under their by-lines."

Red Barrett looked up from the press table nearby and grinned. "Coming from anybody else, we'd be insulted, McGarry," he said. "But we know you love us."

McGarry made a rude remark in reply and then turned back to Bill. "Anyway, Oakley was feeling badly enough about the guy getting hurt. Not that he was hurt very badly – a few stitches around his upper lip. But you know, Oakley is a clean player. . . . Anyway, in comes this Blake and walks up to Oakley. Right after we'd come into the room, Ott Tihane had got Oakley aside and told him not to say much about it no matter what. Because when a thing like that is hot, sometimes it gets in headlines the next day and then there's a feud that lasts for a whole season. 'Get dressed and get out of here,' Ott had told him, and that was good advice, but somehow this Blake got in and he said to Oakley, 'Did you do it on purpose?' "

McGarry laughed, "You know Oakley, he wouldn't say fudge if somebody dumped a pail of it over his head, but I guess he was just feeling worried enough himself that he really got mad. 'What do you mean?' he yelled at Blake. 'What do you mean? Do you think I'd tell you if I did do it on purpose?' "

McGarry shook his head. "Of course, that's the worst thing he could have said! All he had to do was say 'No, of course I didn't do it on purpose,' and that would have been that. But he has to go and yell that if he had done it on purpose he still wouldn't say so, and of course, that's the way it comes out in Blake's broadcast the next day. And then, oh boy, the fuss. People writing letters to the editor saying that if this was the kind of brutality they had in the National Hockey League, it wasn't much better than bullfighting, and all that jazz."

Suddenly McGarry seemed to sense that he wasn't in exactly the area that was going to make Bill's mind any easier. "If I were you," he said, "I wouldn't listen to the guy. If he says something nasty it will make you feel worse, and if you don't hear it you just won't know what it is."

Red Barrett had been listening to this from the press table. "That's why McGarry never learned to read," he said to Bill. "He never wanted to find out what a lousy hockey player he is."

McGarry picked up his bowl of blueberries and made a motion as if he were going to throw it. The lady up where the food was put both hands up to her bosom as if she were going to faint. Bill looked over her head to the clock. He got up. Butt rose with him. "Where you going to listen?" Butt asked as they pushed their way through the swinging door.

Bill said, "My room."

Butt said, "I'll come too."

Bill thought, that isn't the way he'd normally say it. Normally, he'd wait around sort of shyly to see if he was going to be asked. He must be taking this pretty seriously.

Upstairs, the voice of a news announcer faded

in giving the weather forecast. Then, after a commercial, there was some rousing band music and Hanson Blake's voice followed immediately. "This is Hanson Blake with news from the world of sport," he said. The band music welled up for a few seconds and then faded back again; the voice resumed.

"I guess many of you have heard by now that Benny Moore, the tempestuous young defenceman who is trying to make a place with the Toronto Maple Leafs, was badly hurt in a game last night in Peterborough. I was at that game and saw the play in which he was hurt.

"Now to fill you in a bit on the background: Moore has a bad record in hockey. Hitting an official with a puck during last year's junior playoffs brought him a suspension. He went to the Toronto camp on sufferance, but the suspension, which was imposed by the major junior hockey league and upheld by the National Hockey League, was lifted in time for that game Tuesday.

"You've heard also that Moore and a brash young rookie from Winnipeg, Bill Spunska, have been feuding ever since the camp opened."

At the words "brash young rookie," Butt looked at Bill. Some other players had drifted into the next room. Rupe McMaster had come in from next door, and Buff Koska from down the hall. Jiggs Maniscola came in and so did Steve Baldur. All the chairs were gone when Ron Stephens came along. He sat on the floor. All this was during the opening few remarks and they all listened intently.

"Spunska is about the same size as Moore and a couple of years younger, but he hasn't had anything like Moore's training in the game. Compared to Moore, Spunska is crude and unpolished. But he is big and strong, and he seems to think that's enough to carry him along in this game. . . ."

Butt was flushing slowly. Bill felt as if he had been slugged in the solar plexus. McGarry had come in and parked himself on the end of the bed. "I told you you shouldn't listen to that so-and-so," he said.

But the voice went on. "I haven't been able to find out yet what started the dissension between these two young players . . ."

Bill said, "He didn't ask."

". . . but it's my impression that with so much at stake, Moore would not go out of his way to pick a fight with anybody."

McGarry said, "Oh, that guy!"

"Anyway, as you've heard me say, every time these two have opposed each other in practice there have been some body checks. Big ones! I'd say that they've been about even, although

Moore might have come out a little the worst of it because he is trying so hard to cleanse his record by playing the game cleanly . . ."

Otto Tihane said, "I think we should all put in and get this guy a pair of glasses."

". . . but anyway, last night the culmination of this feud came. There was a loose puck in the centre zone and Spunska and Moore both went for it. Spunska had a jump on Moore, and the puck was along the boards so that he had to cut in toward it to pick it up and then try to go on and make a play on goal. Moore was the only man who had a chance to catch him. He's a smooth, powerful skater, which is just the opposite of the way Spunska skates. Spunska went in toward the boards after that puck as if he was going to go right through the boards, and then turned at the last moment and saw Moore. At least Spunska said he didn't really know it was Moore, but you can make up your own mind about that. When he saw Moore coming toward him, he used a trick that many of you have seen before. While reaching for the puck, he crouched a little and then with exact timing came up powerfully to crash into Moore as Moore got there trying to check him. Moore's helmet came off and he hit the ice with his head and stayed there. He was carried off the ice by stretcher and was taken to the hospital in Peterborough, where an operation has been performed. He has not regained consciousness and his condition is listed as serious."

At this point Blake paused. Bill sat on a straight chair, elbows on knees, staring at the floor.

"I think in some ways this accident points up the lack of responsibility that is part of the burning desire some youngsters have to make names for themselves, no matter who gets hurt along the way. It has often been said that pro hockey has had very few fatal accidents, compared to other sports. Let's hope this doesn't blemish that record, both for the sake of Moore and for the sake of that young man, Spunska, who now must be wondering whether it was all worthwhile."

Koska said, as the music swelled up, "Kid, he's a nitwit. Forget it."

Bill said nothing. He stood up and shoved his hands in his pockets. He didn't want to act a big, emotional scene, but nothing had hit him as hard in his whole life as the words that radio announcer just said.

How many people would believe him? Bill wasn't experienced enough to know how much credence the Toronto management put in this kind of publicity. But he didn't know yet what Pokesy Wares thought of the play at all.

Otto Tihane said, "I'll tell you something. Moore has his faults, but in some ways he's not a bad guy."

Everybody in the room looked at this veteran with his knobby nose and one ear partly cauliflowered, and the clear, candid blue eyes. "The best way to shoot down that guy Hanson Blake is for Moore to come to and say what I think he'll say. And that will be that he was trying to bash Spunska into the boards, and doesn't know what happened after that."

Some of the players began to drift out of the room. Only Tihane, Koska, Spunska, and Butt were left. Tihane looked at Koska and Koska looked at Tihane, and then the two of them looked at the younger players. "There's a good movie on a couple of blocks away," Tihane said. "Do you young fellows think you can stand to see one more movie?"

Even a day before, Bill would have reacted to such an invitation from these two NHL stars as if it had come from royalty. He recognized the intent. He wasn't enthusiastic. He didn't have to be. Butt jumped up and said, "Sure, let's go."

On the way out Tihane said, "I'll give a call just in case." He dialed the hospital.

When he turned away from the phone his face was noncommittal. "No change," he said.

They got their coats and left. Not once on the

way did Bill think of the old gang at Northwest
and how envious they would be of Bill Spunska
tonight.

CHAPTER 20 ■

At a little after ten that night, Bill was alone in the hotel room. Alone in the room with two beds, two armchairs, a dresser, a fully carpeted floor, and the pictures on the wall. Through the window he could see that the light drizzle was still falling. He could hear the hiss of the tires on the wet street. He had been trying to write a letter home. He knew that the papers there would have something about the accident. Should he phone? He couldn't decide and he couldn't get started on the letter. He had written the date and Dear Mother and Dad, but that was as far as he could go.

Bill rubbed his hand through his hair and wished that he had someone to talk to.

The phone rang and he grabbed it.

"Hello?"

"It's George Wares," the gruff, direct voice said. For a second or two Bill was confused. He'd never heard Pokesy Wares, the coach, called anything but Pokesy before. But he recognized the voice, of course.

"Wondered if you are going to be free for a little while," the coach said.

Bill said, "I'm not doing anything."

The coach said, "Come down here, then."

"When?" Bill asked.

"Right now, if you can."

A terrible thought shot through Bill's mind. "Nothing . . ." he began, "nothing . . . has happened to . . ."

"Moore?" Wares interrupted. "No, and nothing's going to, either. A guy with a head like his . . ."

It was a lame joke and the coach let it trail off. "Come on down."

Bill still wondered what it was about. He stood by the phone for a moment after he had hung up. Then he lifted the receiver again. When the hospital answered, he said, "Any change in Benny Moore's condition?"

"No change," the woman said.

"Still unconscious?"

"Yes. No change."

"Thank you."

He put on his shoes, tied his tie, and slipped on his jacket. He was fairly calm. It was only when he was ready to go to the coach's room that he began to pace again. He had wanted so much to do well at this camp, and now suppose Moore died?

He stood by the bed looking down at a picture of Moore in one of the papers. The photograph didn't have the truculent expression that Moore usually wore. In it, he was simply a dark young man with a square face and rather an appealing straightforward look to his eyes.

The coach's room was much bigger than the ones up on the third floor. The door was open when Bill came along the hall. He knocked and paused, looking across the expanse of carpet. The coach's voice sounded from back in there somewhere. "Come on in."

The coach had been sitting over near the television set. He left it on, at a western. "Want a Coke or something?" the coach asked. He waved over toward the dresser where there was a tray full of Cokes and also a bowl of ice in which rested a quart of milk. "Get me a milk while you are at it," he said.

Bill got one of the soft drinks and filled a glass with milk for the coach. On the dresser was a photograph of a woman and two children, both boys of around thirteen or fourteen. Bill never had thought of Wares as a father or a family man. He was simply a man in a long-peaked cap who knew all there was to know about hockey and was trying to get it across to other people.

"About time for me to have a talk with you anyway," Wares said. "We'd better get a couple of things clear before you let this thing bother you too much."

Bill felt that he was flushing a little. "It *is* bothering me," he said.

"Why?" the coach asked. "Did you do it on purpose?"

"No!" Bill said. But then the questions that had been assailing him all afternoon came to his mind. "I mean, what's . . . how can you tell? We'd been banging each other every time we got a chance for a whole week. Wouldn't I give him a little extra if I knew it was Moore? I wasn't conscious of doing that. But it could have happened."

The coach laughed, a short barking laugh. "Well, you have been thinking about it!" he said. "I'll tell you, kid. You can't afford to think about things like this and play this game. A guy goes by you with his head down some night, carrying the puck, your job is to hit him as hard as you can. You want to do it cleanly, but checking is part of the game. Checking and skating and shooting – that's the game. If you're going to be afraid every time you hit somebody you're going to hurt him, you're not going to be the kind of a hockey player that I've thought you might become, from watching you in the last few days."

Bill said nothing.

The coach got up and paced to one window and then to the other, hands in pockets. His jacket was off and he was wearing a white shirt with a bow tie that was undone, the ends hanging down under his collar. "Maybe it's a little too soon for you to think about this the way I'm going to say it," the coach said. "But I'll have to take that chance. If something happens to Moore, I might not get this kind of a chance to talk to you again. Now, first, my best information is that nothing will happen to Moore.

"I was talking to Jim Murphy just a little while ago. He said Moore seemed to be able to move all right and is showing signs of regaining consciousness. But he might be out of the game for two or three months. He might be out for the season. And he might be out forever. I'm giving it to you straight because I think this is something you have to face.

"Also, I think you have to face the fact that when Moore hit you that first day with his stick and his elbow it could have been you getting carted off that ice. Nobody in this game goes out to kill another guy. But if it happens, you've got to be just like, well, a businessman who competes so hard that he forces another guy out of business. He isn't going to close up his business because of that, is he?"

"I don't know," Bill said miserably. "I just

218

keep thinking that if he's hurt badly, I'm going to . . ." His thoughts trailed off.

"Going to what?" But the coach didn't wait for an answer. "Look," he said. "Since you started showing so well around here I've talked to people about you. Squib Jackson told me about how you approached the game. You come from a well-educated family and your natural course would have been to go to university. You picked hockey for your own reasons. He told me it had something to do with getting rich quick, or getting established quick, or something. . . . I don't know, and I don't care. If a guy's a good enough player I don't care what makes him tick. But whatever you've got, it shows out there on the ice."

Wares stopped in his pacing up and down and stared at Bill. "You're a lousy skater," he said.

"I know," Bill said, and there was a sudden flash of his old enthusiasm. "I'm going to work at it."

"You're a lousy skater!" Wares repeated. "You don't know how to lay a pass over properly! You don't take a pass as well as you should. But you rush well. And you shoot pretty well if that one goal last night was any indication." He paused again. "Was it, or was it a fluke?"

The coach seemed to say exactly what he

thought without buttering anybody up or softening any questions or comments. "I practised shooting all last spring," Bill said.

"Practised shooting all spring, on what?" Wares asked.

"I had an old piece of arborite or something that had been torn off a counter some place when some wreckers were taking down some stores," Bill said. "It had a pretty smooth surface."

"How many pucks would you shoot off it in a day?" Wares asked curiously.

Bill knew exactly, because it had been a task he set himself every day. "Two hundred," he said.

Wares stopped in the middle of the floor, jammed his hands deeper in his pockets, and gave that short barking laugh again. He kicked a footstool out of his way, still laughing. "Two hundred!" he said. "What did you shoot at?"

Bill said uncomfortably, "A couple of us made a sort of a goal out of some old lumber."

Squib Jackson wandered in through the door, in time to catch that last remark. "Get him to tell you about his body-checking machine, Pokesy," he said.

Bill could feel his nose turning red and the red going right up to his hair line. Wares laughed again. "Body-checking machine?"

"Tell him, Bill," the head scout said.

"Well . . ." Bill said, "it didn't work, anyway."

The scout was chuckling now. "These kids got one of those long duffel bags and filled it with sand and hung it from a crossbar in a guy's garage," he said. "It must have weighed two hundred pounds! They'd get it swinging and give it body checks as it went by. Just about killed three or four little guys before they finally gave it up."

With the coach and the head scout laughing, Bill said sheepishly, "It knocked me down a few times, too."

"How long did you have it up?" the coach asked.

"Three weeks," Bill said, thinking of the final uproar when little Benny Wong got hit on the face and broke his nose.

They'd had the bag hung up in Benny Wong's garage. When Benny went in with his nose flattened all over his face, his father came out with a knife, cut down the body-checking machine and dragged it out into the lane and let all the sand out. Thinking of it, Bill began to grin, and he told a little bit of it. Benny's father said the Wongs had flat enough noses without making them any flatter. He thought the coach and the head scout were going to fall on the floor with laughter.

CHAPTER 21 ▬

Tim Merrill moved back into Bill's room that night. He was laughing when he came out of the shower the next morning. "You know, a lot of people that don't know any better look at the kind of lives we lead, and they think we've got it kind of soft. Now, for instance, a guy looks at his morning paper this morning and finds out that we're going to be in Kitchener tonight, and do you know what he thinks? He thinks, 'Those lucky stiffs! Here I've got to go down to the office and slug away at making a living, and those guys probably sleep until noon and then have a big meal and take off and go and play hockey. What a cinch!' "

Bill was calling the hospital. He looked at the town hall clock against the blue September sky outside the hotel room window. Ten to seven. The girl at the hospital said: "No change."

He was usually in and out of the shower pretty fast, but this morning he must have dawdled.

Over the noise of the shower he heard a shout, "You drowned or something?"

He stuck his head out. "I'll be right with you. You go on down."

Tim said okay.

There was no scrimmage in the practice this morning. The defence combinations worked for an hour against incoming forwards. Sometimes it was three-on-two rushes, sometimes two forwards with the puck coming in on a lone defenceman. Bill had trouble keeping his mind on his work. It must have been noticeable to others. King Casey skated over to him once during the workout and stood alongside him. The famous Irishman, one of the finest and fastest-talking defencemen the NHL ever had, was known to have a way with young players. When Wares got some players so mad at him that they could scarcely lace on their boots, Casey was the one who came along and somehow converted the anger into goals. He had a gravelly voice and a colourful way of talking, and everything he said was genuine.

"Don't feel that you're carrying the weight of the world on your shoulders," he said. "Look, kid, Otto Tihane and the coach both told me they tried to get this across to you. Now I'll try. Stop me if you're bored."

Bill had to grin, "Bored!"

"It might happen once or twice a year for the next ten years, or fifteen, if you become a professional hockey player, that you or somebody will get hurt badly. You know as well as I do that a puck in this game might travel a hundred miles an hour. It's a hard piece of rubber, with a sharp edge on it. Also, those hockey sticks aren't padded with foam rubber! When a stick gets a little high, or you happen to fall into one, you can get hurt. And you can sharpen a pencil on the edge of the skates. We've tried to do everything we could to make them safe by putting guards on the ends of them and that sort of thing, but the fact is that when two or three players go down in a pile-up there are sharp skates flailing around there and people do get cut. I'm here to tell you I've been in this game a lot better than fifty years now and I've taken my licks, but I'm safer doing this than walking across streets for a living, and that's the truth."

When he skated away he called back over his shoulder, "Now you start thinking about that game against the Rangers in Kitchener tonight, and don't let one other thing come into your mind."

Back at the hotel he was heading for the pay phone when Pam came out from behind the desk and just took his arm and squeezed it and said, "No change." But her eyes were saying something sympathetic, to go with the squeeze.

They arrived in Kitchener about three. As they were pulling into the outskirts of the city, Bobby Deyell stood at the front of the bus and called out, "Steaks have been ordered for three-thirty. When you get there you'll find the situation at the desk as usual – they'll have room numbers and keys for you, so after you eat you can rest."

The main street of Kitchener was crowded and narrow. Especially beside the hotel where they unloaded. Most of the players had been here before. They got off, stretching and saying hello to a few people who had been hanging around the front of the hotel to meet them. Then they went on inside where tables were set and ready for them. Before they had been there for fifteen minutes they were all eating.

"Going to rest?" Merrill asked Bill as they were going up the stairs after eating.

"I guess I will," Bill said. This custom of having a mid-afternoon steak and then a rest in bed for a couple of hours was a luxury that he'd never had before. In the kind of hockey he'd played, he'd eaten at home and then rushed to get a bus, his stick slung through the loops in his duffel bag and his skates dangling down his back. But he didn't say any of this. Not that it would have been a surprise to Merrill. He'd done it, too. Everybody had.

"I've got some friends here," Merrill said. He

made a couple of phone calls and then while Bill stretched out on one of the twin beds, he put on his coat and said, "See you later."

Left alone again, Bill wished there was some way of knowing how Moore was. He thought of the game tonight. What would happen when a man came in on defence and should be body-checked? Could he body-check anyone, any more?

The next thing he knew the phone rang and he grabbed it. It was dusk outside. "Hello?" he said.

"It's Tim," the voice said. "It's a quarter to seven. Coming? Two or three of us down here are going to get a cab."

Bill said, "I'll be right down."

The lobby was crowded. He walked swiftly, eyes straight ahead, to the door where Tim was waiting. They walked across the sidewalk and he heard a man say to his wife as they passed, "That's Tim Merrill. The kid with him – hey, that must be Spunska, the one who just about bumped off Benny Moore!"

A few kids got autographs from the players as they piled out of the cabs. The dressing room was quiet, players slowly getting out of their clothes. The two goalkeepers, John Bosfield and Ed Hill, were sitting together on one bench. Hill was in his underwear, tugging at the buckles and straps of his goal pads with the air of a foot soldier inspecting his foxhole. He never talked before a game. Bill didn't think Hill had said anything to him since this camp started. Now Hill looked up and said hello, almost jovially. Jim Butt stopped by a minute and said, "Those UBC guys are here tonight." They were the ones putting together the Olympic team. It seemed a year back to last Saturday on the way to the game in St. Catharines when he'd read about their being interested in Jim Butt and Zingo Zubek.

Bill found his place on the bench. His equipment was topped with a clean sweater of Leafs' road uniform. He hung up his coat and jacket in the locker and sat down and began to loosen his tie and looked down at the planks beneath his feet. His stomach, or something inside him, sank and hardened and twisted into an ache at the thought of going out on the ice again. What was the matter with him, anyway? Why couldn't he remember what King Casey and Otto Tihane and those others had told him? He kept his eyes down, putting on his uniform automatically. The other players came and dressed and undressed and chattered and exchanged insults with each other and the trainers. Bill leaned over to tape his leg guards into place. He did this and other things mechanically, progressing with his preparations for the game. But now that a game was near, action in earnest, it was as if Moore had been hurt just now instead of nearly two days ago. He was scared.

The coach didn't have much in the way of a pep talk before they went out for their warm-up. He said, "If you guys are going to get anywhere this year, this is one of the teams you've got to beat every time you play against them. Starting tonight."

They went out and worked through the warm-up and came back. The older pros took off their skates immediately and sat for the next few minutes in their sock feet. Then the time came a few minutes before eight when they started putting their skates back on. The conversation was stepped up a little – with just a hint of nerves and jumpiness in it. Then the buzzer went and they all jumped up to go out. Ed Hill, who was going to play the first thirty minutes of the game, went first. Then Jiggs Maniscola, Jim Butt, Koska, Tihane, Annie Oakley, McMaster, McGarry (talking). The rest. Bill fell in near the end of the line. When they walked to the ice they were met with scattered boos. There was one shout from the seats along the rails. Everyone could hear the booming voice. "Who are you going to put in the hospital tonight, Spunska?"

Buff Koska said dryly, "At least they're starting to know your name, kid."

In the Rangers' warm-up Bill had picked out

young Patch Kachure, a lanky, earnest-looking kid that he'd seen play junior hockey in Winnipeg last year and who had been drafted by the Rangers. Kachure was lashing shots at Jim Crozier, the thin and bald New York goalkeeper.

Bill was on the bench as the game began, the Oakley line with Stephens and McGarry against Steve Buckoski, the Rangers centre who had been an all-star last year. In the Toronto goal, Ed Hill's mouth was open and he was yelling, although in the other noise at the start of the game Bill couldn't hear what he was saying.

Maybe Wares wanted to find out right away how Bill was going to react. He had five defencemen with him – Merrill, Tihane, Koska, Baldur, and Spunska. Koska and Merrill had started. On the next shift Bill heard the voice behind him saying, "Spunska and Tihane! Get ready!"

Then Bill and Tihane were moving at their own blueline, watching a rush come in from the Rangers.

Bill knew from the first play. There was a face-off at the other blueline. The referee blew his whistle and dropped the puck and faded back out of the way all at the same split second. Annie Oakley slapped Buckoski's stick away and got a pass over to Stephens on the right boards and then moved in on the Ranger defence looking for a return pass. It came. But the puck hit a skate and deflected hard into centre zone, toward the Leafs' blueline. Buckoski raced back for it. Bill was a little slow in starting for it but they both got there at almost the same time. Buckoski had his stick far ahead of him to try to pull the puck in to his control. For that instant as Buckoski stretched for the puck he had his head down and even the old Bill Spunska of the high school league in Winnipeg would have given him the full thrust of his shoulders, chest, and legs in a crushing body check. He would have had the puck, Buckoski flattened, and he would have been in on the Ranger defence and the heat would have been on.

All this went through his mind in the split second that Buckoski, open and vulnerable, was within range.

Johnson, the bull-necked youngster on the Ranger defence, saw it too. Although it would have been much too late, he yelled, "Heads up!"

But Bill hadn't thrown the check. And Buckoski, getting the puck to him, pulling it away from Bill, looked up and saw the danger he'd been in and on his face appeared a look first of surprise and then of contempt for a rookie who didn't know a chance to make a check when he saw one.

The coach of the Leafs had seen it, too. Bill

could hear his yell above all the others, just one brief disgusted word.

As the game warmed up, Bill found that sometimes he could forget. Sometimes he couldn't. If it was a matter of two or three players going into a corner for a puck, he could shove and pull and poke at the puck with the best of them. Man to man, it was different. Once or twice he had a chance to throw a check but did so indecisively, weakly, trying to envelop the other man instead of knocking him to the ice.

Still, Wares kept him on a regular shift. The coach came along behind him once and stood there the way he did when he was going to speak. Then he went away. The sweat rolled down Bill's forehead and face. The murmurs along the bench came to him. This was where he wanted to be but he had to play better hockey than this to do it! He was the one who knew it.

In the second period there was a yell from the crowd as he eased a Ranger into the boards so gently that the Ranger, thirty pounds lighter than he was, knocked him down!

"Gun-shy!" roared a man in the crowd. "He got Benny Moore and now he's gun-shy!"

Bill turned quickly and looked toward the voice and saw that a girl up there was turning to look at the man who was yelling – and the girl was Pam!

In the intermission between the second and the third periods, the coach was waiting for him just inside the door. "In here," he said, jerking his head toward a tiny room off the main room. Bill clumped in there. The coach followed him and closed the door. They were alone.

"You're playing a lousy game," Wares said, looking straight into Bill's eyes. "I should tell you to take off that uniform and we'll drop you at the Toronto airport on the way back to camp – and you can come back when you've grown up a little."

Bill stared at him. Wares was holding his eyes, and the coach's eyes were hot and angry.

"And that's what I'm going to do," the coach said, almost casually, "unless you show me in the third period that you want to play hockey and stop using that accident as a crutch."

That was all. Wares turned, walked through the door, turned again, walked out of the dressing room, and slammed the door. None of the other players looked at Bill when he walked through the dressing room. He sat with his elbows on his knees, staring at the wooden floor. He thought of two years ago when he had first started to try to play hockey, the people who had tried to help him, then and since. Was he going to throw it all away, for an accident?

Would that help Benny Moore? Or help any-body?

Those few quiet minutes he recognized later as among the most important in his life. He did not entirely accept that it could happen to anyone, that it happened every day somewhere, that sticks were hard, pucks flew fast, and skates were like razors. That was all true, but. . . . That was the big but; he had to be sure of his intent. He had not been sure in the Moore incident. That had been the trouble.

From now on, he said to himself, *I not only won't hurt anybody on purpose in this game – but I'll try, on purpose, not to hurt them.* He thought of the way Tim Merrill played: hard, strong, forceful, but never dirty. He thought: All those things that have been said about me really are being said about the worst side of the game. There has been doubt sometimes in the past whether so-called accidents really have been accidents. But for as long as I play the game, I want people to think of me as a clean player. Names of other players, famous in the NHL, came to his mind. All clean. Some all-stars. A man could be an all-star, and be clean.

That would be him, Bill Spunska.

It was a long, sober thought for a boy not yet nineteen. When he rose, he felt as if his whole body was electric. Other players noticed, and looked at one another, but said nothing to him.

The coach noticed and put him on the first shift. It was a hunch, and Pokesy Wares had lived on hunches all his life.

And once again there was a rush on the Rangers' end, with the Leafs driving in. A pass was picked off, the puck lifted into the centre zone. Steve Buckoski raced for it. Bill had been playing up and had to come back to head him off. Now Buckoski had the puck but Bill had improved his angle. Both skating flat out, Bill poked for the puck and missed. When he missed he followed through with his shoulders and body. Buckoski went down, not gently. Bill, turning, saw him getting up again. Then Bill was driving like a fullback in on the New York defence. The crowd was roaring. His wings were at the defence. He did what the coach had said he did well – the low, hard shot. He was wide open as he did it and down he went, hard. He slid along the ice on his seat, watching the goalie save on his shot, but send the rebound straight out to Annie Oakley. There was the shift this way, that way, open air, the shot. And the red light for a goal. When he went to the bench the only mention Wares made was a terse, "Now you're talking." Nothing more.

It was enough. It was the first goal of the game. Leafs eventually won it, 5–2.

Pam had come down with Mrs. Koska. "I would have told you we were coming but I wasn't sure I could get off," she said. Several wives had driven up from Toronto for the game. When they were eating later, Tim Merrill took Bill over to meet his wife. She was pretty and blonde. Their five daughters were with her and she looked as if she could be one of them, instead of the mother.

Pam and Bill were talking with Squib Jackson and another scout in the next booth when a man came in from the hotel desk and looked around. "Mr. Wares!" he called. "Telephone."

The coach got up and went to answer it. At first Bill scarcely noticed. An NHL coach seemed to spend half his time on the phone. But when the coach came back there was something about him that suddenly made Bill sit up. He came straight to Bill and Pam.

"That was Jim Murphy," he said. "Moore has come to, for keeps. He said that all he remembers is that he was going to knock Bill here right through the boards when suddenly the lights went out."

"He's okay?" Bill asked.

The coach grinned. "He's okay. You'll be able to go and see him yourself in a day or two." He turned to Squib. "Will you call the newspaper and radio guys and tell them exactly what Moore said? That should end this thing."

Bill and Pam stood there. They turned to each other. There was no hesitation. They came together with a sigh, holding each other tightly. They pulled back a little and looked at each other and the happiness in their eyes was not all relief about Benny.

It lasted a good five seconds before Squib Jackson cleared his throat, grinning. "What's the name of the friend of yours in Winnipeg, Bill? Ah, Sarah? . . ."

"You dirty so-and-so, Squib!" Pokesy said, laughing.

Bill and Pam looked at each other. Bill somehow knew, or at least was sure (who could really know?) that this was not what he and Sarah had had. But that was something to be worked out later. He needed more time to think.

"I'll call Sarah and let her know about Benny," Bill said. "She was worried."

They all looked at him. The chuckling dwindled away. Pokesy was the first one who spoke. "Cool," he said. "No bleeping wonder you're a good defenceman."

CHAPTER 22 ━

The Friday morning workout had been going for ninety minutes, maybe a little more, when there was a whistle and the coach called for a change of defencemen. The big rink was nearly empty and every sound echoed. The lights shone down on ice that was becoming chewed up from the hard usage. High behind the seats some windows were open and the sunny sky showed outside, and when Bill came off with this player change he let himself fall over the boards into one of the rail seats and for a few seconds looked at the sky.

He had hoped it would rain. No such luck. The Leafs' annual golf tournament would be played this afternoon. By custom, every player in camp competed. Bill had never even swung a golf club. He had prayed for rain. Now it seemed that nothing could save him . . . and how those guys would laugh! He grinned to himself to think of it, and switched his attention back to the ice, watching every move intently. He'd never realized until these last few weeks how much there was in hockey that he simply didn't know.

A voice behind him said, "Hi, kid."

He turned to see Red Barrett, his favourite of the hockey writers in camp. Red had his hat pushed back on his bald head and that quizzical look on his face.

At first Red's bluntness had seemed to Bill to be grumpiness, or bad temper. But now he knew it was just bluntness. With Red, you knew where you stood. He'd given up calling him mister after the first few times, because each time Red had said gently, "Call me Red."

"Hi, Red," he said now.

"You know yet where you're going?"

Bill said, "No." He knew further cuts would be made today. "Do you know?" he asked.

"I got an idea."

He was gone before Bill could ask him, "Where?" Bill realized that Red probably had hurried off on purpose, to forestall the question. He watched the ice, but from the corner of his eye he noticed Red's destination. Halfway up the side of the rink was a little group of men. Managers and coaches and scouts in the Leafs' system. Writers and radio men. And two or three men that Bill hadn't seen before.

Whistle on the ice. Line change. Bill went over the boards, fresh and ready. He was like that, he found. Some other players stayed tense when they came to the bench. He just seemed to collapse all over, inside and out. A minute or so of that kind of relaxation and he was as fresh as if he were just starting out.

The coach came to him and Ott Tihane.

"Block the blueline," he said. "Make 'em pass, make 'em swerve, hit 'em."

Face-off was in one of the red circles down by the other net. This was five men against six, a penalty situation. Bill's side, the Blues, was short one man. The Whites – wearing the white cotton jerseys over their regular sweaters – got the draw. Maniscola was picking his way out, passing up. The penalty killers were back-checking furiously. A pass went to Jim Butt. He cut in to centre. Bill and Tihane crowded the blueline. Jim passed. Bill intercepted. McGarry ragged the puck in centre ice. It was checked away from him. The Whites came again. Bill missed a check, was caught out of play. Goal. Whistle. "Stops and starts," the coach called. The usual groans. Bill and Jim Butt did their stops and starts together. Bill could beat four others on the team now. But he lost a foot or two to Jim every time. Start, skate as hard as you could, stop at the blueline, skate hard through centre, stop at the other blueline, skate hard to the end of the rink, stop in a cloud of ice chips, turn, do it again.

Finally, one more whistle. Once around the

rink as hard as they could go. Then off. Some
players skated directly to the boards and leaned
there, resting for a few seconds, before they
straggled off the ice.

Jim and Bill were at the gate leading off the
ice when Bill noticed the coach leaning over the
boards, looking their way.

Bill had a strange feeling. He's decided, Bill
thought. He's going to tell us now.

The coach called out and moved up to the
second row of seats, his baseball cap pushed
back. Beyond was the main group of official
and semi-official watchers who now would wait
for St. Catharines to come on the ice and would
watch them, too.

The coach grinned at Bill and then at Jim. "I
never thought you kids would be around this
long. Did you?" They didn't say anything and
Wares chuckled. "Anyway, the time has come.
The curfew tolls the knell of parting day and all
that stuff. I got a proposition."

Bill now knew – as he had known all along, in
his secret heart – that the Leafs were beyond
him, now. But how about St. Catharines?
Where else was there? A junior club, like the
Marlboros in Toronto? Or the Peterborough
Petes? Or back to Winnipeg?

The coach was speaking directly to Jim. "You
know that a couple of fellows from the Univer-

sity of British Columbia have been trying to get you, eh? For the Olympic team?"

"I read about it," Jim said. Bill noticed there was no mention of what the coach had said after the exhibition game in St. Catharines: refusing to let the men talk to Butt there.

"What do you think?" the coach said.

Jim grinned. "I'd rather be with the Leafs."

The coach smiled back. "If you get off your butt – that's a joke, son – and work for the next few years, you might make it, too." He turned to Bill. "Same goes for you, and you'd better listen to the rest of this. They want you, too."

He went on talking. Bill stood there, stunned. Phrases of what the coach was saying came through the fog. Whatever courses they wanted, they could take. Must get good grades. If they wanted to turn pro after the Olympics, they could. "If you're good enough!" Could carry on with extension courses wherever they happened to be, if they wanted. Room and board and tuition. Jobs available to provide spending money.

And then the coach stood there, looking from one to the other. "There weren't any chances like this around when I was a boy," he said mournfully. "Or maybe I would have wound up the only coach in the NHL who was also a psychiatrist! Officially, instead of just unofficially!"

"For me, too?" Bill said unbelievingly.

"You, too," said the coach.

Bill thought: I could stop in Winnipeg on my way out there. See Sarah and Pete and the family a day or two. They'd be glad about the university. And so would I! An Olympic team! He realized that he'd thought about it quite often in the last week or so. Often with a thought for the luck of such as Jim Butt and Zingo Zubek, wanted for something like that. Imagine playing on the same team as Zingo Zubek! He laughed and some players chatting with friends nearby looked at him curiously.

There was a twinge of regret over leaving the Leafs. But . . . next year. Or the next.

"Count me in," Bill said.

"When do we leave?" Jim asked.

The coach turned and yelled up to the group of men in the stands. "Hey, they're all yours – for two years! Just don't spoil 'em."

And then Jim and Bill stood there while two men detached themselves from the group and began to come down the steps, slowly, toward them.

The following morning, they were let in to see Benny Moore. He was wearing a bandage like a white helmet. His grin was his best one.

"Pam told me what you're doing," he said.

"I'm sorry about this," Bill said, gesturing to the bandages.

Benny kept right on grinning. "You better keep your head up the next time you come in on me, Spookski," he said.

Jim said, "How long are you going to be in here?"

Benny said, "They tell me I'll be out in three weeks and skating a month later. *If* I feel strong enough. They might even let me play in St. Catharines late in the season. . . . Olympic team!" He looked at the two of them. "Hey, could you imagine Benny Moore on an Olympic team?"

They couldn't. But they said they could.

At the bus depot at one o'clock, Pam came to see them off. And Tim Merrill. Buff Koska. Merv McGarry. Jiggs Maniscola. A delegation.

"Hey!" called the woman behind the cigarette counter, the one who had spoken to Bill that first night. "Going, eh, Spunska?" She knew his name, now. "Well, you seem to have made some friends anyway."

Bill and Jim got on the bus. Pam kissed Bill good-bye. McGarry shook hands with the bus driver, Bill, Jim, Pam, and the lady behind the cigarette counter. The others called, "Good luck!"

The bus started. As it rolled out of town, Bill

settled deep into his seat. Looking at the blazing autumn colours of the maples and oaks they were passing, he began going over these last two weeks, almost a day at a time, and thinking of what he had learned. Not all about hockey. Not at all, all about hockey.